"Kelli, I'm going to kiss you," Logan warned her.

"Why? You don't even like me," she answered, her voice shaking slightly.

"Liking you has nothing to do with it."

She frowned. "You thought I belonged in a home for demented fairies."

A smile touched his lips. "I still do."

"And I should allow you to kiss me after that comment?"

His finger reached out and tenderly outlined her mouth. "I don't remember asking your permission."

"Why, you . . ." Her voice faded as Logan slid his hand behind Kelli's head and drew her closer.

Her arms slipped around his neck and a sigh escaped her as his lips settled on hers. He pulled her firmly into his arms. Logan's heart went into double time. Was she feeling the same magic he was?

WHAT ARE *LOVESWEPT* ROMANCES?

They are stories of true romance and touching emotion. We believe those two very important ingredients are constants in our highly sensual and very believable stories in the *LOVESWEPT* line. Our goal is to give you, the reader, stories of consistently high quality that may sometimes make you laugh, sometimes make you cry, but are always fresh and creative and contain many delightful surprises within their pages.

Most romance fans read an enormous number of books. Those they truly love, they keep. Others may be traded with friends and soon forgotten. We hope that each *LOVESWEPT* romance will be a treasure—a "keeper." We will always try to publish

LOVE STORIES YOU'LL NEVER FORGET
BY AUTHORS YOU'LL ALWAYS REMEMBER

The Editors

LOVESWEPT® • 427

Marcia Evanick
Satin Sheets and Strawberries

 BANTAM BOOKS
NEW YORK • LONDON • TORONTO • SYDNEY • AUCKLAND

SATIN SHEETS AND STRAWBERRIES
A Bantam Book / October 1990

LOVESWEPT® and the wave device are registered
trademarks of Bantam Books, a division of
Bantam Doubleday Dell Publishing Group, Inc.
Registered in U.S. Patent
and Trademark Office and elsewhere.

If you would be interested in receiving protective vinyl
covers for your Loveswept books, please write to this
address for information:

Loveswept
Bantam Books
P. O. Box 985
Hicksville, NY 11802

ISBN 0-553-44058-6

Published simultaneously in the United States and Canada

Bantam Books are published by Bantam Books, a division
of Bantam Doubleday Dell Publishing Group, Inc. Its trademark, consisting of the words "Bantam Books" and the
portrayal of a rooster, is Registered in U.S. Patent and
Trademark Office and in other countries. Marca Regis-
trada. Bantam Books, 666 Fifth Avenue, New York, New
York 10103.

PRINTED IN THE UNITED STATES OF AMERICA

OPM   0 9 8 7 6 5 4 3 2 1

To Cathy S.

Friends are like panty hose.
It's always nice to have ones that
support.

Thanks

One

Kelli SantaFe slid the last bobby pin in place and studied the effect of her costume in the full-length mirror. It was perfect. Not only was Ruth a genius with cookie dough, she sewed a mean fairy outfit. In fact it was her finest creation to date. When Ruth insisted on buying two dozen scarves in shades varying from pale pink to rose at a flea market, Kelli had had some doubts. Then when her friend had bought an exercise leotard in pale pink, Kelli started to panic.

Seeing her reflection in the mirror now, she knew Ruth's instincts were right. The scarves were sewn together diagonally at the waist so the hemline of the outfit reminded her of teeth on a saw. The longest point did not quite reach her knees. A pair of pink tights and clear wings completed the outfit.

Kelli's eyes strayed to the deep vee of the leotard and smiled ruefully. Well, not all fairies could be seductive, she supposed. Maybe she'd try for the wholesome look.

She braided her long golden hair with rose-colored ribbons and pinned it up on top of her head, then pulled open a shoe box full of makeup. She'd give Ruth and Henry the full effect.

She had just finished applying rose-colored lipstick when the doorbell rang, playing the first notes of "We're Off to See the Wizard." The doorbell rang for a second time before she was halfway down the stairs. "Whoever it is, is impatient," she muttered. Ruth and Henry would have let themselves in. So maybe it was Josh.

By the time Kelli reached the door both the third string of notes as well as her good mood were fading. She angrily pulled open the door and snapped, "Yes?"

Outside the door, Logan Sinclair's mouth fell open in astonishment. He knew this place was called Fairyland—he had passed the signs proclaiming: FAIRYLAND—ENTER AT YOUR OWN RISK. OWNER NOT RESPONSIBLE FOR MISCHIEVOUS DEEDS DONE BY FAIRIES—but he didn't expect a ravishing fairy to answer the door.

Hallucinations brought on by jet lag, he told himself. He was definitely having hallucinations.

Logan shook his head and stared at the fairy again. Maybe it was jet lag combined with the shocks he'd received in the past forty-eight hours. And he had had a series of shocks. When he'd arrived at his aunt and uncle's, he'd discovered the house had burned down months earlier. The neighbors had assured him that Ruth and Henry were fine and living with their nephew Edwin. But from there things had turned from bad to worse.

When he arrived at Edwin's, he'd learned that his second cousin had abandoned his aunt and uncle at a tourist trap called "Fairyland." Even though Edwin had tried to reassure Logan, telling him the couple was gainfully employed, for the past hour he had envisioned dark dungeons and holes in the ground, with his aunt and uncle chained up and treated like animals . . .

Kelli saw the look of astonishment on the face of the man standing on her doorstep. He was gorgeous, a little frazzled looking, but wow! She'd buy whatever he was selling.

The man was just shy of six feet with tousled light brown hair, streaked with blond highlights. He appeared to be in his mid-thirties, with broad shoulders and rugged good looks. Kelli decided that when she died she wanted to be reincarnated as a cotton plant to be made into a pair of jeans for this man. The worn denim that hugged his thighs had to be happy. She smiled invitingly at him. "I'm Logan Sinclair," he said. "I'm looking for my aunt Ruth and uncle Henry."

With those words Mister Gorgeous turned into a toad. With instinct born of too many years fending for herself, Kelli batted innocent gray eyes. "Who?" she asked. Logan didn't notice her hand slip up the door frame to flip on a hidden switch. Instantly sounds of a fierce growling dog filled the living room.

Kelli noticed Logan's hesitant step backward and she closed the door, leaving only an inch of space. "Down, Killer. Go behave yourself. Bad doggie," she called over her shoulder. "I think you have the wrong house. I've got to go. Killer seems a little upset."

The door was about to close when Logan jammed his foot in. Kelli looked down at the offending Nike and saw a strong tanned hand grip her doorknob.

A silent battle raged between the handsome stranger and the fairy princess guarding her castle.

Logan was beginning to admire the strength of

the willful fairy standing before him, when the barking halted abruptly and an ear-piercing train whistle rattled the cottage windows. He watched the fairy cover her ears and utter an obscenity.

She reached over quickly and pressed the stop button on the tape player next to the door. *Okay, so plan A didn't seem to be working.* That left out-and-out war. She might be small, but she could hold her own.

With the strength of desperation, she tried to close the door. "They're mine and you can't have them," she shouted.

His original assumption had been correct. They must be locked in the basement. Logan caught the door and pushed against it, finally inside her house. "Do you go get them or do I look for myself?" he said calmly.

Kelli caught her bottom lip between her teeth. She knew physically she was no match for him. Now what?

The next moment Ruth entered the room and screamed "Logan!" and flew into his arms. Kelli watched as Logan closed his eyes in relief. She felt a twinge of guilt for her selfishness but quickly buried it. This was war.

As Ruth dabbed her eyes with her apron, Kelli made her move. She grabbed Logan's hand and started to shake it. "It was really nice seeing you, Logan. As you can see your aunt is just fine. Why don't you stop by again around Christmas. With the holidays and all, we just love company."

She had almost led Logan out the door when he realized her scheme. "Who in the hell are you?"

"Logan, don't swear like that in front of Kelli," said his aunt.

He looked at the girl dressed in the strange costume. "You're Kelli?" When she nodded, he asked, "Where're your parents?"

Kelli narrowed her eyes in warning.

"Logan, where are your manners?" Aunt Ruth asked. "Kelli owns this place. She's my boss."

"As of this minute you quit." He turned back to Kelli. "You should be ashamed of yourself, making people my aunt's age work. My aunt and uncle should be enjoying their golden years. Not scrubbing your floors."

"Logan!"

"Aunt Ruth, go pack your bags this minute. We're leaving. We're going home."

Kelli looked at the two of them. She realized maybe she didn't have to fight. She'd give Logan enough rope to hang himself. "Where's home, Mr. Sinclair?"

"What?"

"Last I heard, you lived somewhere between a harem and a duchess's boudoir."

Logan's jaw fell open as he faced Kelli. "Who told you that rubbish? I've never been inside a harem."

"But obviously you have been in a duchess's bedroom," Kelli said triumphantly.

Logan was clearly at a loss for words. He turned to his aunt. "What have you been telling this elf?"

"She's not an elf, she's a fairy, dear. I didn't mean to tell her; it was that drink at the party."

"Drinking? Party? Just what in the hell is going on here, Aunt Ruth? I leave the country for one year and when I return I find you and Uncle Henry living in a fairy commune attending wild parties."

"It wasn't a wild party," Kelli said indignantly.

"No, no, dear, it wasn't a wild party. At least not until the police came. You should have seen Henry's face when the officer tried to handcuff him."

"Oh, my Lord! That's it. Aunt Ruth, go pack

your bags, we're leaving immediately. Where in the hell is Henry?"

Kelli started feeling a little sorry for Logan. The explanations did sound pretty terrible. "I sent Henry to rescue Mustardseed," she said. "She's caught behind the waterfall."

Logan sighed. "I'm going to regret this, but who is Mustardseed?"

"She's my cat; she thinks she's a fairy," came the innocent reply.

"Great, just great." Logan ran his hands through his hair. He was losing patience. "You sent a seventy-two-year-old man out to rescue a cat-fairy from behind a waterfall?"

"Of course. He's done it many times already. Henry knows all Mustardseed's tricks by now."

Mad. They were all stark raving mad. "Look, Miss Kelli Fairy, this whole place is loony. I am taking my aunt and uncle out of here immediately. Then I'm going to catch about ten hours of sleep. When I wake up, I'm going to the police and have this place closed down."

Before Kelli could protest, Ruth spoke up. "No wonder you're so cranky, Logan. You haven't been getting your proper rest. You know how you always become a little difficult when you don't get your nap."

"I don't need a nap," snapped Logan. He was truly exasperated now.

"Of course not, dear, I'll go make you a nice cup of hot cocoa. You always loved my hot cocoa before you took a nap. It will calm your nerves. Your latest assignment must have been a humdinger." With a click of her tongue, Ruth headed for the kitchen.

Logan stared at his aunt's retreating back. "I don't want hot cocoa," he said loudly. "I don't *need* a nap. All I want is to go home!" He had traveled halfway around the world, with layovers in places that weren't even on maps, to come home. To him home wasn't a particular set of four walls, it was a feeling. Home was the feeling he shared with his aunt and uncle. A feeling he didn't share with fairies.

For the first time Kelli stopped and really looked at Logan. Dark circles lay under his brown eyes. His skin was drawn tightly over his cheekbones and every line on his tanned face was pronounced.

"Logan?" Kelli asked gently. "How many hours have you been up?"

He gave a start of surprise. She seemed to be asking a caring, reasonable question. "Why?" he asked evasively.

"Because I really think you're too old to whine. It's not a pretty sight. Besides, you're not making much sense."

"I come home to find my aunt and uncle living with Peter Pan in Never-Never Land, my uncle possessing a police record, and you owning a cat that thinks it's a fairy. All I'm waiting for is a crocodile that ticks and we'll be all set." He gave her a look of contempt then addressed the ceiling. "And she thinks I'm not making sense."

"You keep shouting for Ruth to go pack her bags, that you're taking her home. Well, in case you haven't noticed, this *is* their home." With a weary sigh Kelli sat down on the edge of the couch, leaning forward so she wouldn't crush her wings. "The crack about the crocodile was low, really low."

Logan gave a small smile. "I'll take back the crocodile crack if you take back the whining remark." When all he received was a raised eyebrow he conceded, "Okay, maybe I did whine." He tried to hide a yawn behind the back of his hand and took a good look at the room. At first glance it was a very normal-looking living room. Two faded blue chairs didn't quite match the couch. A worn red rug lay in front of a wood-burning fireplace that seemed to be the cottage's only source of heat. A narrow staircase led to the upper floor. Just off the living room, Logan could hear his aunt bustling around in the kitchen.

But the piece that made the room unusual was on the far side of the room. An old china closet, lovingly polished to a high sheen, held bizarre contents. Artfully displayed on handmade doilies were doorknobs: some were brass, others seemed to be of pewter, while still others were porcelain with hand-painted flowers. One or two appeared to be made from colored glass. The most promi-nent doorknob was pure crystal that reflected an array of colors.

Well, maybe there was a logical explanation for the doorknobs. Since his aunt appeared un-harmed, he decided to give her the benefit of the doubt.

"So, Kelli, do you have a last name or didn't they give you one when they pulled you up from the cabbage patch?"

Kelli jerked as if he'd hit her, and she rose slowly to her feet. "I had a note pinned to me saying my name was Kelli, and the nurses at the hospital named me SantaFe. I was named after the city where I was abandoned." Slowly she made her way to the stairs. "Now if you'll excuse me, I think I'll go change."

She was halfway up when Logan came to his senses. "Kelli, wait!"

Before Kelli could respond, Ruth called Logan for lunch.

With a flat voice Kelly said, "Go get your lunch, Logan, before it gets cold."

Logan stood and watched her climb to the top. Part of him wanted to follow her and apologize—another part thought he should wait until she came back down. When Ruth called his name again, he headed for the kitchen. Logan told himself she'd be down in a minute.

But a nagging little voice in the back of his mind reminded him that fairies were famous for disappearing.

When Kelli descended the stairs twenty minutes later, she could hear an argument in the kitchen. Perhaps it couldn't be called an argument, she thought, since only one person was raising his voice. Logan. She felt a little guilty for eavesdropping, but his voice *was* loud and it was her house. "Living with a fairy doesn't constitute a home," Logan told his relatives. "Maybe an asylum, but not a home."

"Never judge a fairy by her wings," Ruth replied.

Kelli bit back a grin.

"Why didn't you write to me when your house burned down?" Logan demanded.

"We did, Logan, three times," Henry said. "The first two letters Edwin mailed for us. The last one Kelli mailed herself to the U.S. Embassy in Istanbul."

"Istanbul?"

"Wasn't that where you were?"

"No. I was working in Khartoum."

Ruth's astonished gasp was clearly audible in the living room. "Oh, my. Where's that?"

"Sudan."

"No wonder we couldn't find you, son," Henry said, in wonder. "Ruth told me Istanbul."

"No, Henry, I *told* you I *thought* it was Istanbul. All I could remember was there were a lot of letters and it sounded foreign."

Kelli couldn't hold back a giggle.

"Why didn't you contact the corporate office?" asked Logan, truly exasperated.

Kelli entered the kitchen. Calmly she poured herself a cup of coffee and grabbed a handful of oatmeal cookies.

"All the phone numbers and addresses you gave us were lost in the fire," Henry said. "We knew you were an archaeologist or something. Someone who likes to dig around in the dirt."

"Geologist." Logan looked at his aunt and uncle and realized how old they'd become. For the past ten years he'd traveled around the globe. Always before he'd ended his assignments at their house. They were his home base, his only family, except for his distant cousin Edwin, whom he'd always disliked. As he looked at their faces he noticed new lines, edged alongside the old ones. Ruth's glasses seemed thicker and her hand trembled slightly, but love still shone in her blue eyes. Henry's shoulders were stooped and there wasn't quite as much white hair as Logan remembered, but he wore a dark green cardigan that looked new. Where had he been when all these changes were taking place? In some foreign country searching for oil. "I'm a geologist. I work for one of the top oil companies in the world."

"There goes my Indiana Jones fantasy," Kelli said, sighing.

Logan glanced up. Worn jeans, sneakers, and a baggy red sweatshirt had replaced the enticing pixie outfit. With her blond hair pulled back into a saucy ponytail and her face free of makeup, she looked around twenty-five instead of eighteen. He saw laughter lurking in her hazel eyes. He knew she was laughing at him. "Do you mind? This is a *family* discussion."

Ruth and Henry gasped in shock. Kelli stared into her coffee. Tears stung the back of her eyes, but she refused to blink. She should be used to that type of comment. She'd heard enough of them in the endless array of foster homes she was shuffled through.

She'd been sixteen when Ben caught her living in one of the outbuildings on his property. The property she owned now. For no apparent reason except that they needed each other, they became family. She was the daughter he'd never had; he was the father she longed for. Child welfare had labeled her an incorrigible runaway, and they were happy to see Ben Williams apply to be her foster father. But by the time she was twenty she was alone again. Ben had died of emphysema at the age of fifty-six, leaving her his entire estate of nineteen acres, five run-down buildings, a livable cottage, and a pile of back taxes and bills.

For the past five years she had built and nourished Fairyland, an outdoor park that boasted leaf-covered walks, two small waterfalls, a pond, and an outdoor theater. When Ruth and Henry were left on her doorstep last October, she adopted them as family. She finally had grandparents.

She looked at Logan, sadly. He was right, the three of them were family. Kelli felt like an outsider in her own kitchen. She drank the last of her coffee, pocketed the cookies, and headed for the back door. "I've got work to do. Have a nice chat."

Logan quickly rose to his feet. "Kelli, wait!"

When she hesitated by the door, he ran fingers through his hair, desperately trying to think of what to say. "I am sor—"

"Logan, you should never apologize for telling the truth." With her chin held high and her back straight, Kelli closed the door behind her and headed for the woodshed.

Logan pulled up the collar of his blue windbreaker and shivered. The March afternoon was turning bitterly cold. After a year of extreme heat, his body was finding it difficult to adjust. In the distance he heard the hum of a chain saw. A frown tugged at his mouth as he pictured Kelli wielding the heavy machine. It seemed too dangerous for her.

He headed into the woods, following the faraway sound. He had forgotten how clean the air smelled in spring and how beautiful barren trees could look as they sported tiny new green buds. Everywhere he looked held the expectant air of rebirth. Tiny shoots were breaking through the damp soil and anticipation fairly sang in the trees as birds rapidly flew about looking for building materials for their nests.

As he crossed over a wooden bridge spanning a small creek, a smile of appreciation curved his lips. He followed the path toward the chain saw noise, hoping it led to Kelli. He owed her more than an apology. He owed her his thanks.

Logan rounded a curve in the path and stopped. Kelli was bending over an enormous log, and with the expertise of a lumberjack, was slicing it into a manageable size. Afraid that any movement from him would startle her, he stayed perfectly still and watched, fascinated. Plastic safety goggles protected her eyes from the flurry of flying wood chips. The blade was practically through the log when she brought it back up, and with her left leg pushed the log a quarter turn and finished the cut.

The screaming saw quieted to a low roar as she positioned herself for the next cut. Logan took one step closer. A large old English sheepdog raised its head and barked.

Kelli heard Tinkerbell's bark over the roar of the saw and looked up. Logan. She muttered an unladylike oath, turned off the saw, and lowered the safety goggles to hang around her neck. After placing the saw on the ground, she reached for the thermos lying in the bottom of a rusty wheelbarrow. She watched, amused, as Logan eyed her dog. Tinkerbell weighed about seventy-five pounds, but with her thick shaggy hair she looked closer to a hundred. Presently, she was lying on the ground in a crouched position. Her teeth were bared and her eyes, one blue and one brown, were gleaming. To a stranger she looked ready to attack. Kelli knew the dog was really smiling.

Perhaps he'd suffered enough. "Tinkerbell wouldn't hurt a fly," she said. She saw him relax and start forward. "You leaving already?" Not waiting for a reply, she continued, "Have a nice trip and don't forget to write."

"I'm not leaving. Aunt Ruth invited me to stay."

Kelli studied the thermos clutched in her hand. She had known this was coming, so why wasn't she prepared for it? This was now Ruth and Henry's home too; they could invite guests to stay if they wanted to. But why Logan? Why the one person who could spoil her newfound happiness—the person who could take her family away? She reminded herself again what Ruth had told her about Logan. He never stayed long. Sometimes it was a two-day visit; the longest was two weeks. Kelli could handle anything for two weeks, even Logan. As long as he cleared out *alone*, leaving his aunt and uncle behind.

"It's Ruth's home too."

"But you own it."

She raised her chin. "Are you asking my permission?"

Logan glanced around, uncertainly. It went against the grain for him to ask permission to stay with his aunt and uncle, but he wasn't positive they would leave with him—yet. They liked living here and had become very attached to Kelli SantaFe in the past five months. Common courtesy required he ask her consent. "Yes," he said, "I'd like your invitation."

Kelli knew what that request must have cost him. He obviously loved his aunt and uncle very much if he had agreed to stay in an elf village. She wanted to scream "No, you can't stay," because he was the enemy, but her common sense told her Ruth and Henry would probably follow Logan if she pressed the issue.

She looked at him and smiled. "You may stay as long as Ruth and Henry like. Why don't you go get some shut-eye, you look beat."

"Thanks. They offered me a bedroom in the house."

"Ben's old room?"

"Yes. They said there wasn't any room at their cottage." Logan saw a disturbed look cross her face. "Changed your mind?"

Kelli had no option. Ruth and Henry shared a microscopic cottage about a hundred yards behind her house. Their cottage consisted of one large room that was kitchen, living room, and bedroom combined. She'd recently added a small bathroom and closet for their comfort. It really was impractical to expect Logan to stay there with them when there was an unoccupied room in her house. "You can stay." She pulled up her goggles and turned back toward the log.

"Kelli?"

She looked over her shoulder. "What?"

"Can we talk for a minute?"

"Listen, Logan, you're dead on your feet and I've got work to do. Why don't you get some sleep and we'll talk later."

"I want to thank you for what you've done for Aunt Ruth and Uncle Henry."

"I didn't do it for thanks."

"I know." He kicked at a rock. The woman before him was small and compact, not quite five feet two. Her eyes were hazel, her nose had a slight slope, and her mouth was a trifle large for her face. She wasn't beautiful, by current standards, but her skin held a healthy radiance. Wood chips clung to every inch of her body, and he had to suppress a desire to brush them off.

For the past two hours Aunt Ruth and Uncle Henry had told him the story of how Kelli had rescued them from Edwin. Edwin had begrudgingly taken them in after they lost everything they owned in the fire. It was supposed to be temporary—only until the insurance company came through. But the insurance company had claimed they had no record of their policy, and their copy had been lost in the fire.

Five weeks after they moved in with Edwin, he had taken them for a drive to give his wife, Suzette, a break. When Ruth saw the sign for Fairyland, she'd asked to stop. The story became fuzzy at this point, but the end result was they had moved in with Kelli that very day.

Logan sadly shook his head at the picture she made with one foot on the log, goggles protecting her eyes, and one delicate hand clutching a chain saw. She was so tough on the outside, so soft in the middle. Anyone who would take in an elderly couple must be a pushover. He wondered why she put on such a tough front. He regretted that he was going to cause her more pain. "I'm sorry, Kelli," he said. "When I leave here, my aunt and uncle will be coming with me."

Kelli pulled her goggles away again and studied him. The shadows beneath his eyes were even more pronounced and his shoulders sloped wearily, but he still radiated authority. Logan Sinclair was a man to be reckoned with; a man who knew what he wanted, and got it. The only thing was, he now wanted what she desperately needed—her family.

She lifted her chin, pulled back her shoulders and faced her opponent without a trace of fear. "I think Ruth and Henry are old enough to make their own decisions." She put on the safety glasses, brought the saw back to life, and tore into the log lying at her feet.

Logan silently congratulated her courage. If she'd screamed, shouted, and thrown him off the property, Ruth and Henry probably would have followed out of loyalty. But she opened her home to him, told him he looked like hell, and said the decision was Ruth and Henry's to make. How was he supposed to fight that?

With a weary sigh he headed back toward her house. Obviously it wasn't time for any major discussion. He'd catch up on his sleep, plan some strategy, and then confront the fairy queen.

Two

Logan awoke feeling that someone was watching him. He slowly opened his eyes and stared at the nightstand next to the bed. Less than a foot away crouched the largest cat he had ever seen. Its fur seemed to be a pale gray and its golden eyes shone in the darkness. Could this be Mustardseed? he wondered. The cat certainly didn't look much like a fairy.

The clock in the red Buddha's stomach on the nightstand showed it was five-thirty. With a sigh, he realized he must have slept through the night. Logan kept a cautious eye on the feline as he slipped naked from the bed and headed for the shower.

He closed the bathroom door behind him and glanced around curiously. Yesterday he'd been too tired to take in much of his surroundings, but after fourteen hours of sleep he was refreshed. The room was white and had huge ferns and palms painted on three walls. The fourth wall was taken up by a claw-footed tub with a brilliantly colored parrot on the shower curtain. The mural was so vivid Logan felt as if he were standing naked in a conservatory. Not only was the painting well done, it somehow suited the cottage—and Kelli. A small flash of red on the wall caught his attention. Near the floor, behind the door, was a signature. Curious, he knelt and read the one-word signature. Kelli.

That Kelli had painted the mural didn't really surprise him. What did was that her signature was dated six years earlier.

He turned on the water and stepped beneath the pounding warm water. So far Kelli was an enigma. He liked to pigeonhole people into little boxes. Everyone he knew fell into a certain category and there they stayed until something happened in their lives to make him change their box. It made life easier.

But Kelli didn't fit into a box. She was a puzzle, and he didn't have all the pieces yet. He chuckled. He didn't even have all the *corner* pieces yet.

He slowly turned off the shower, dried, and reached into the medicine cabinet for his razor. His hand was on the can of shaving cream his aunt had unpacked for him, when he noticed how empty the cabinet was. Where were all the cosmetics, perfumes, and endless tubes of lipsticks? Where were the moisturizers, hair removers, nail polish, emery boards, tweezers, and the thousands of items that most women crammed into a bathroom cabinet? The only items on the four wide shelves were a pink disposable razor, toothpaste and brush, a roll-on deodorant, and a small bottle of baby oil. The middle shelf held all his items and the top shelf had a brush, comb, rubberbands, and a Dixie cup full of Q-Tips. He raised his chin and carefully ran his razor up his throat. Kelli SantaFe was still an enigma.

*   *   *

The sun was high in the sky and breakfast was over by the time Kelli rolled from her bed. She tripped over Tinkerbell and headed for the shower. Twenty minutes later she and Tinkerbell walked into the kitchen only to find Logan and Ruth enjoying a cup of coffee. She mumbled "Good morning," before heading for the coffeepot sitting on the stove.

Logan watched Kelli pour herself some morning brew and smiled. This morning she wore a pair of tight faded jeans and a red sweater that emphasized more than it concealed. Her hair was pulled back from her face with two barrettes and dangling red beaded earrings swung against her delicate neck. A pair of dark sunglasses were perched on her nose and electric red socks covered her feet. He wondered why she wore sunglasses at eight-thirty in the morning, especially in March.

"Good morning, Kelli," he said. "Sleep well?"

Kelli bit back a tart response. She had fallen into bed at five o'clock and her alarm had sounded at eight. Three lousy hours of sleep. She remembered the exhaustion that had lined Logan's face the previous day and suppressed a snappy reply.

She yawned daintily. "Like a baby." She reached into a Garfield cookie jar and handed the shaggy dog at her feet a bone.

"Your pancakes are in the oven," said Ruth.

"I've told you before, Ruth, please don't cook breakfast for me. You know I'm not a big eater in the morning."

"I didn't cook them. Logan did."

"Oh. Thank you, Logan. Since you are Ruth and Henry's guest, feel free to help yourself to anything in the house. But you didn't have to cook breakfast." She walked over to the back door and picked up a pair of brown leather boots that had seen one too many winters. "I have to run off. I have a meeting that I'm going to be late for if I don't hurry. Thanks anyway, Logan, for the thought." She downed half the cup of coffee and pulled on the boots.

Ruth handed Kelli a handful of cookies from the teddy bear cookie jar. "Eat these on your way."

"She can't eat those for breakfast," Logan said. Kelli smiled.

"Why not?" demanded Ruth.

"Because I've made her buttermilk pancakes."

Ruth pulled herself up and glared at her nephew. Her ample bosom puffed out the plain flowered cotton housedress she wore. "I've been making those oatmeal cookies especially for her for the past five months. And she loves them, don't you, Kelli?"

"Yes, Ruth, I love them. I love all your cookies. Now both of you knock it off. I've been taking care of myself for years and I haven't died of malnutrition yet." Smiling, she said, "Thanks again, Ruth, for the cookies." She kept smiling as she faced Logan. "Thanks again, Logan. If I weren't in a hurry, I would have eaten your pancakes. I'm sure they are delicious. But the cookies are great, just like eating a bowl of oatmeal." She pulled on an old leather bomber jacket that had probably seen World War I, and shoved her arms in and zippered it to her chin. "Now you two behave and have a nice visit."

"Will you be home for lunch?" asked Ruth.

"No. I'm meeting Josh in town for lunch. I'll be back sometime this afternoon." With a farewell pat to Tinkerbell she opened the door.

"Well, you have a good time, and tell Josh I'm making a batch of brownies tonight. Maybe he'll stop by."

"I'm sure he will," said Kelli, laughing.

Logan watched the back door close and glared at his aunt. "Who's Josh?"

With a sparkle in her eye, Ruth replied, "Why, Josh is a dear friend of the family. You really must meet him, Logan."

Logan answered the back door. His aunt and uncle were finishing up the dinner dishes. "Yes?"

"You must be Logan Sinclair, Ruth and Henry's nephew. I'm Josh Langley."

Logan looked at the man standing before him. He disliked him on the spot. From common courtesy, he shook the offered hand. "Come on in. I believe we're expecting you." When Josh entered the kitchen, Logan's displeasure turned to hatred. The man was perfect. Coal-black hair, crystal-blue eyes, and gleaming white teeth shone in a model-perfect face that Hollywood would die for. Logan frowned as he noticed Josh's dark blue police-man's uniform, complete with shining silver badge.

For the first time in his life, Logan felt threatened by another man. Unreasonably threatened, he knew. He'd held his own against some pretty steep competition for the affection of the few ladies that visited the oil fields.

Henry turned from the cabinet he was putting plates into and smiled. "Hi, son. Knew you would come as soon as you found out Ruth was baking brownies."

"Hi, Henry. How's it going? You didn't split that pile of wood outside, did you?"

"Lord no, boy. Logan did that around six this morning."

Josh turned to face Logan. "Thanks. I would have gotten to it this weekend. Where's Kelli?"

Logan forced a smile. "I think she's in her workshop. I'll go get her." He grabbed his windbreaker from the rack by the door and headed out into the chilly evening. He followed a path around the back of the house and headed to the dilapidated building Ruth had pointed out earlier as Kelli's workshop. He didn't know how it was still standing. The roof was sagging, paint was peeling off in strips, and two windows were cracked and held together by masking tape.

Both Kelli's house and the small cottage where Ruth and Henry lived were clean and in good repair. Nothing indicated wealth, but there weren't any signs of neglect, either. With a grimace of distaste he knocked on the warped wooden door.

No reply.

Gingerly he opened the door and spotted Kelli. She was seated near a kerosene heater, with her dog lying beside her. Her back was toward the door and she appeared to be carefully painting the yellow tutu on a statue of a fairy. There were a pair of earphones over her head and she was softly humming along with the radio. In distress, he noticed the three sweatshirts and the black knit fingerless gloves she wore. He closed the door behind him, but could still feel a draft move through the shack. How could she work in these conditions? he wondered. "Kelli?"

She didn't reply and Tinkerbell appeared to be sleeping. He took two steps further into the run-down shack. Shelves constructed of planks and cinder blocks held concrete statues of fairies, similar to the one she was painting. Two propane lanterns, the only source of light, hung from wires attached to the ceiling. The concrete floor was cracked, patched, and splattered with paint. Two more windows graced the back wall. One was undamaged, the other had a piece of plywood nailed over it.

But, astonishingly, the room was clean. There wasn't a cobweb or speck of dust in sight. A wastebasket held a paper bag half full of trash and a broom was propped against the far wall. Logan cleared his throat and called her name again. "Kelli."

Kelli saw Tinkerbell raise her head. Without turning she knew someone was in the room. Tinkerbell was half deaf and relied mainly on sight to alert Kelli to visitors. She turned, saw Logan, and gently pulled the headset off. "Is there something I can do for you?"

Inexplicably, the anger shot through him. She was acting sweetly and politely toward him again. And Mister Uniform was waiting for her in the kitchen; all Josh needed was a telephone booth and he'd probably change into Superman. "Lover boy is here."

One fine golden brow arched. "Who?"

"Josh Langley. You know, the guy who chops your wood and meets you for lunch."

Kelli was unsure why he sounded so sarcastic; she decided the best thing to do was ignore it. "Thank you, Logan. I'll be right in."

Frustrated at her lack of response, he demanded, "What's he to Henry?"

Kelli dropped the paintbrush into a container of water and placed the eighteen-inch statue on a shelf. "They're friends. Being so far from town, Henry doesn't get a chance to talk to other men.

Whenever Josh visits they talk about fishing and stuff."

"Do you know that Henry calls him son?"

She slid the can of paint onto a shelf with a dozen other cans. "Sure. Is there something wrong with that?"

"He only calls me that," he said, knowing he sounded unreasonable.

Kelli finally realized that Logan wasn't as sure of himself as he pretended. He was worried that Josh was replacing him in his uncle's heart. She smiled with understanding. "Try to understand what was happening. Your aunt and uncle were taken in by a complete stranger. They'd never met me before the day they moved in here—"

Logan quickly interrupted. "I don't understand how that happened. Would you please explain to me how you got Aunt Ruth and Uncle Henry?"

"No. That concerns your family. All I can say is I ended up with them, and I've never regretted it." From his stubborn expression, Kelli knew the subject was far from over. "About a week after they moved in," she said, "I threw a party, just a few friends and the drama department. The party was in full swing when Josh showed up with his grandparents. We thought it would be nice for Ruth and Henry to meet other people their own age."

"Was this the party Henry was arrested at?"

"Henry was never arrested. Josh showed up directly after work wearing his uniform. To the delight of your aunt and the entire drama department, he pretended to arrest Henry for drunkenness and disorderly conduct. Henry never laughed so hard in his life and they became fast friends."

"Okay, maybe I overreacted. Josh seems like a nice enough guy."

Kelly pulled off two sweatshirts and hung them on the back of the door, along with the gloves. She turned down the kerosene heater to low, opened the door, and extinguished the lanterns. "Josh *is* a nice guy." She walked out the door and watched as Tinkerbell ran off into the surrounding woods. "Henry told me he called Josh 'son' because he reminded him of his nephew, Logan, whom no one seemed able to locate."

Sheepishly, Logan trailed her into the kitchen. Half an hour later he had to admit she was right, Josh was an okay guy. Between the brownies and coffee they talked about fishing, gardening, and Fairyland.

"So Kelli, what's the first play going to be?" asked Ruth.

"*A Midsummer Night's Dream.* The local school district is required to perform a classic, and it's a tradition to do the Shakespeare comedy in May. In June they will be doing *Rumpelstiltskin* and in July the group will perform *The Tempest.* Then they'll top off the season by doing *Peter Pan* in August."

Ruth clapped her hands in excitement. "I can't wait. Do you think I could sit in on the dress rehearsals?"

"I'm sure they won't mind. But don't tell them you know how to sew, they'll rope you into making some costumes," said Kelli.

"Oh, I would love to help them." Hesitantly Ruth asked, "If that's okay with you, Kelli. It is your sewing machine."

Kelli stood up and refilled her cup, looking away from the others. "How many times do I have to tell you Ruth, you don't have to ask my permission for anything. This is your home too. If you want to use the sewing machine, be my guest. I just don't want to see you overworked, that's all."

"Gracious, child, me overworked? I haven't done anything more strenuous than bake cookies since we moved here."

Logan glanced from Kelli to Ruth. "I agree with Kelli. Don't overdo it, Ruth."

Josh watched the silent exchange and quickly changed the subject. "Henry, how would you like a fishing pole? My dad was cleaning out the attic and found three rods up there. He's keeping one, and one is pretty old. But there's a real nice one he is going to sell at the garage sale next month. He's asking only two bucks for it. I could bring it over this weekend and you can see if it's worth it."

"Two dollars, heh?"

"That's what he said," Josh replied as he picked up another brownie and bit into it.

Logan watched as Kelli gave Josh a full one-hundred-watt smile that lit up the room. She looked ready to jump out of her chair and throw herself on Josh. Logan frowned. Kelli never smiled at him that way. She was always courteous and polite. Almost overly polite. But then why *would* she smile at him? He never offered Henry a fishing pole for two bucks. He could go out and buy him a brand-new rod, but Josh did one better. He'd offered Henry his self-respect by allowing him to make a financial decision. While Logan would be offering charity.

Kelli smiled at Josh, silently thanked him for the fishing pole. Since they lost everything in the fire, Ruth and Henry were living on Social Security and a small pension check. The bulk of their money was spent on doctors and prescriptions. Ruth had a chronic heart ailment, which was only partially covered by their insurance. The remainder of their funds was spent on clothing and a few household incidentals.

Kelli had discovered they were a proud, stubborn couple who refused any charity. Between Josh, the senior citizens club they had joined, and flea markets, Kelli had managed to help them furnish their small cottage, but she was running out of ways to trick them into accepting any luxury items. For the past five months she had been writing, calling, and threatening the insurance company that Ruth and Henry swore had held the fire insurance on their modest ranch house. By now she wasn't sure if the company was trying to wiggle out of paying the claim, or if Ruth had actually forgotten to pay the premium.

She was startled out of her wandering thoughts when Josh announced he was leaving. "I'll be back Saturday and I'll bring that pole with me."

"That would be great, son. Fishing season opens next month and I was wondering what I'd be using." Henry smiled.

"I'm sure this pole will do nicely," said Josh. "Kelli, why don't you get your coat and walk me to the car?"

"Sure." With a questioning look at Josh, she put her coat on and zipped it up.

"Come on, Ruth, it's time we were heading home too," said Henry.

Logan finished his coffee. "I'll walk you two to your cottage. I haven't had the official tour of the inside yet."

The dessert dishes were piled in the sink, brownies were put away, and everyone headed out the door. Kelli watched as Logan trailed behind his aunt and uncle and disappeared around the back of the house. Her attention turned back to

Josh, who was leaning against the side of a police cruiser.

"Want to talk about it?" he asked.

Kelli chuckled as she hopped up and sat on the front fender. "About what?"

"Logan Sinclair."

With her eyes on the back corner of the house, she asked, "What's there to talk about?"

Josh shoved his hands deep into his pants pockets. "It's worse than I thought."

"What is?"

"Logan, Ruth, Henry, and you."

"You lost me somewhere, Josh. What are you talking about?"

"Nothing."

"Nothing?"

"That's the point," muttered Josh. "We've been friends for nine years and for the first time you're not talking."

"There's nothing to talk about," she said, slightly exasperated with the conversation.

Josh looked up, studying the stars. After a few moments of silence he quietly said, "He won't take them."

"He wants to."

"He seems like an okay guy. A little quiet, but I guess that's understandable." When the silence stretched out again he added, "Listen, Kelli, he's a traveler. Hasn't he spent the past ten years traveling and working in foreign countries?"

"That's what Ruth told me."

"All he wants is to know Ruth and Henry are fine. Once he sees how happy they are here, I'm sure he'll head back to Istanbul or wherever he came from."

"He thinks I'm a few cards short of a full deck."

"I tend to agree with him," said Josh, laughing.

He tenderly reached up and ruffled her hair. "You don't need those cards anyway."

Kelli slid from the fender as she muttered, "Thanks."

Josh pulled his keys from his pocket and walked around to the driver's door. "How come I've got this feeling Logan didn't particularly like me?"

"Henry calls you 'son.' Logan was feeling threatened until I explained that Henry only called you that because you remind him of Logan."

"That makes sense, but I think there's more to it than that." Josh climbed in his car, shut the door, and rolled down his window. "You know how to reach me if you have any problems."

With a friendly smile and a salute, Kelli said, "Yes sir, dial 911."

Chuckling, Josh called out, "One of these days, Kelli, your glamour isn't going to work," as he drove out of her yard.

Kelli smiled as she watched the disappearing red taillights. Josh was right. What *would* Logan do with Ruth and Henry once he needed to return to work?

"So he's not lover boy."

"Lord, Logan," gasped Kelli. "Must you sneak around in the night?"

"Sorry. I didn't want to interrupt anything."

"There wasn't *anything* to interrupt." She reached for a silver chain that hung around her neck and blew a dog whistle. There was a flurry of barking and then Tinkerbell, covered with leaves, reappeared. "Good girl," she said, laughing.

Logan helped pull leaves and twigs from the matted hair of the animal. "Does she follow you everywhere?"

"Only for the past six years." With a smile Kelli

headed for the warmth of the kitchen with Logan following.

Logan closed the back door behind them and took off his jacket. "He did call you glamorous."

She chuckled. "Next time you eavesdrop, pay attention to the words. He said my glamour."

"Same thing."

Kelli filled the sink with warm water and detergent. "Glamour is the magical power of a fairy."

Logan picked up a dish towel and started to dry the mismatched cups and plates. "Do you have this 'glamour'?"

"Only a fairy has glamour."

"And you're not a fairy."

Kelli dried her hands on a towel. "Do I look like a fairy to you?"

Mischief shone in his brown eyes as they gazed from her worn boots, up past jean-encased thighs, over the soft roundness of womanly breasts covered by the bulky red sweater, to the suddenly shy expression in her eyes. "I don't know. I've never met a real fairy before."

"Take my word for it, I'm not a fairy."

Logan closed the cabinet door and hung up his towel. "You might be; you've certainly bewitched Aunt Ruth and Uncle Henry. They think you're the best thing since Santa Claus and they love it here."

She chuckled as she filled Tinkerbell's bowls with food and clean water. "I love it here too. Only a witch can bewitch someone. Fairies use their glamour."

"No magic wands?"

"That's a human misinterpretation. Fairies don't need wands. They use a thought process that humans don't understand to do their deeds of kindness."

He watched as she opened two cans of cat food and forked it into a large dish, next to Tinker-bell's. "Only kindness?"

"I'm afraid not. Fairies tend to pull mischievous pranks on humans. They feel we are not only stupid but clumsy."

"Sounds like an interesting group. Is that food for Mustardseed?"

"Yes, and Cobweb and Moth too."

Logan followed her as she turned off the kitchen light and headed into the living room. "Who are they?"

"We have three cats here at Fairyland. They are named after the fairies in *A Midsummer Night's Dream*."

"One was in my room this morning. He was pale gray or white and the largest cat I've ever seen."

"That's Moth. Cobweb is a dark gray and Mustardseed is an orange tiger cat. I feed them, but nobody owns them." Kelli hid a yawn behind her hand. "I'm sorry, Logan, but I've got to get some sleep. Make yourself at home. There's no television, but there are plenty of books up in your room that you might find interesting."

"I looked through them this morning. Some of them looked fascinating, others weird, and then some were over my head. I gather they must have been Ben's."

Kelli started up the steps. "Yes. Good night, Logan, and whatever you do, don't lock the doors."

"Why?"

"You're in Fairyland now. Fairies are very curious creatures and take exception to being purposely locked out." She saw Logan's look of disbelief. "Don't worry, they won't harm you, they're just nosy."

"Are you saying there really are fairies?"

"I'm not saying anything of the kind. All I said was don't lock *my* doors."

After she'd gone into her room, Logan stared at the empty stairs and frowned. All day long he'd been revising his opinion of Kelli SantaFe. He had berated himself for jumping down her throat yesterday and for insinuating she was loony. After talking to his uncle and aunt and seeing how happy they were here, he admitted he might have misjudged her. She seemed perfectly normal during dinner, and even her friend Josh was ordinary.

Now all of a sudden she told him not to lock the doors because fairies roamed the house at will.

He turned off the living room light and slowly made his way to his room. He closed his door and headed for the packed bookshelves. Little guys dressed in red caps and curly-toed slippers might be easier to handle than the unbalanced Fairy Queen sleeping in the next room.

Three

"Good morning, Logan. Breakfast will be ready in a minute," his aunt sang out.

"Thanks, Aunt Ruth, but you didn't have to go to any trouble. I can fix my own."

"Nonsense. I love to cook and Kelli's never around to enjoy it." She piled a stack of French toast onto a plate and slid it in front of him.

Logan reached for the maple syrup. "Speaking of Kelli, where is she?"

"She just left to check on her swans."

"Swans?"

Ruth poured herself a cup of coffee and sat down. "Oh my, yes. A pair of trumpeter swans live at the pond. Kelli thinks they are going to have babies this spring. When they arrived last year, the male, Angus, had been hurt. Kelli took him to the vet. The vet removed a bullet from his wing, but he'll never fly again. His mate is Caer, and they make a lovely pair. So graceful."

"Are they named after fairies too?"

"Yes. Angus was the son of the Dagda, High King of the Tuatha. Caer was the daughter of

Ethal Anubal, who was King of the host of Connacht, and her mother was a fairy. Caer was a mortal woman one year, a swan the next. Angus so loved her that he gave up his mortal body and became a swan to be with her."

Logan smiled as he listened to the story. Chalk another one up to Kelli. She had his once sensible aunt believing in this romantic drivel. "Where is the pond?"

"Follow the creek until it forks. Take the path toward the right and it will lead you to it." A smile played at the corners of Ruth's mouth as she finished her coffee. She watched Logan place his dirty dishes in the sink and reach for his coat.

"Take it easy the rest of the morning," he ordered.

"Easy? I haven't done anything except hard-boil eggs for salad and make breakfast for you and Henry."

"Who cleaned the living room? It wasn't like that last night when I went to bed."

Ruth stood and quickly started washing the few dishes in the sink. She looked uncomfortable. "I don't know."

Logan froze, one arm in his coat. "You don't know?"

A muffled "No" was heard above the rush of water filling the sink.

Logan stared at his aunt's back. There was a reasonable explanation. "Kelli must have cleaned it."

Ruth started to scrub down the counters.

"Was she up when you came in?" he asked.

"No . . . Henry and I came over around six-thirty. Kelli woke up about seven."

"I went back downstairs at one in the morning to look for a book and the living room had newspapers piled on the floor and dust on the furniture. Are you trying to tell me they magically cleaned themselves?"

"I'm not trying to tell you anything. I said I don't know who cleaned them."

Logan studied his aunt's stubborn expression and shook his head. He knew from past experience that when she wore *that* look, she was impossible to budge. He didn't believe that rooms automatically straighten themselves, and Ruth obviously wasn't going to help him solve this mystery. But Kelli *could* and *would* answer his questions. "Okay. Let's drop the subject. I'm going for a walk. Where's Henry?"

"He's at the theater marking trees that have broken limbs or need to be taken down."

"Does Henry use the chain saw?"

"Gracious no," laughed Ruth. "If he even held one, it would shake his dentures right out of his mouth."

"Who does all the cutting?"

"Kelli mostly. Josh and some of the students help out on the weekends."

"Well, since I'm here, for now, I guess I could help out."

"That would be nice. Kelli works so hard around here." A mischievous sparkled gleamed in Ruth's eyes. "Just last week I was telling her that we really could use a man around here. There's nothing wrong with Henry, mind you, but a strong, younger man would put some kick into this place. I told her it was none of my business, but she really isn't getting any younger, and she should give marriage some serious thought."

Logan groaned. "Don't even think of playing matchmaker. I told you years ago that I won't put up with it. I'm a grown man who handles my life exactly as I please. So don't go giving Kelli any ideas!"

Ruth looked wounded. "I wasn't thinking of *you*, Logan. I think Josh would make a perfect husband for Kelli." She lowered her head, to hide the gleam of triumph shining in her eyes. "*You* would never do."

The next words were out of Logan's mouth before he could stop them. "Why not?"

"Because she would need someone who was here, not digging up bones in Afghanistan."

Frustrated, he jerked open the door and breathed in the cold air. "I'm a geologist. I don't dig up bones and I have *never* been to Afghanistan, but you are right. I'm never around when anyone needs me."

From the window above the sink Ruth frowned as she watched Logan's shoulders slump as he headed into the woods.

A string of explicit curses tinted the cold air bluer as Logan headed toward the pond. Whatever had possessed him to open his big mouth? What did he care if Aunt Ruth was trying to throw Kelli and Josh together? With a savage kick he sent a rock flying into the creek. It wasn't any of his business.

Logan came to the fork in the path and headed right. If and when he decided to get married, he would make the perfect husband. He might be a little pigheaded at times, but his wife would understand and love him for it. He smiled, self-assured. He was headed toward one woman who would never know how perfect he could be. He would rather be seventy years old and digging up bones in Afghanistan than tied to a woman who still believed in the tooth fairy.

The sight of crystal-blue water sparkling in the bright morning sun caused Logan to pause. The pond was larger than he had first imagined. A half-dozen Canadian geese floated lazily by a weathered lopsided dock on the far side of the pond. A brilliant flash of red caught his attention. Fifty yards in front of him sat Kelli. She was dressed in her old boots, bomber jacket, and a pair of worn jeans. A thick red knitted band held back her flying blond hair and kept her ears warm. A tender smile curved his mouth as the soft melody of a lullaby reached his ears. Kelli was singing to the large white swan who was lying with its head resting in her lap.

Kelli gently smiled at Caer as she tenderly stroked the great bird's feathers and sang. Angus was proudly standing guard in the rough lean-to Kelli had constructed for them. Safely behind him was the bird's pride and joy. Five whitish eggs lay nestled in the large nest at the back of their home.

It had taken Kelli ten minutes of singing softly before she could coax Caer off her nest. Now the bird snuggled closer to her and basked in her accomplishment—motherhood. Kelli was just about to segue into her rendition of "Silence Is Golden" when a twig snapped behind her. A flurry of activity erupted. Caer practically flew back to the nest while Angus dove for the kill.

Kelli scrambled to her feet and spotted Logan. The two furious swans were angrily hissing. "Logan, get back," she yelled above the noise of the birds. She saw him hesitate. "Please, Logan. I'll meet you at the fork in the path in five minutes."

Logan stared at the angry male swan and agreed retreat was the safest course of action. How could such a lovely bird have such a vicious nature? Without breaking eye contact with the swan, he backed up the path, putting a safe distance between them before turning around to walk back to the fork in the path.

Several minutes later, Kelli wearily sat down next to Logan on an old tree stump. "Good morning, Logan. How's it feel to still have both your feet?"

He gingerly wiggled his toes. "Lucky."

Kelli allowed a small smile to curve her lips before she frowned. "Obviously I forgot to mention the swans to you. They're off limits. Caer just laid five eggs, and you already met the proud papa, Angus. Normally they are not aggressive, but under the circumstance I'm sure you understand."

Logan studied her wind-tossed hair and rosy cheeks. Her skin glowed in the bright morning light and her lips were slightly turned down at the corners. He a had sudden urge to kiss that pout away. How would a fairy queen kiss? he wondered. Would it be as soft as a butterfly's caress, or as consuming as a raging inferno?

He tore his gaze from her appealing lips and stared off into the surrounding woods. What was he thinking? How could he even contemplate kissing Kelli? She was the enemy. She held some magical power over his family, and he wanted them back the way they were. Now, without even lifting an eyebrow, she was using her "glamour" on him. Well, it wasn't going to work. Normally he wouldn't even be attracted to her; not that she wasn't beautiful, not that she didn't have a body worth fantasizing about. But she was totally unbalanced.

His voice was harsh with self-disgust. "Sorry. I won't bother the swans again. I only came to ask you if it's okay for me to help Henry cut down some limbs or trees."

Kelli heard the harshness in his voice, and looked at him, bewildered. "Can you use a chain saw?"

"Of course," snapped Logan.

Puzzled by his sudden ill mood she gentled her voice and said, "Thank you. The saw, gas, and safety glasses are in the shed behind the house."

Logan stood up and glared at her. Where was her backbone? Here he was practically shouting at her and she meekly thanked him. Her large hazel eyes looked at him, confused. An overwhelming desire to pull her into his arms and comfort her raced through him. He shoved his hands deeper into his pockets instead. "You don't have to thank me. I'm only earning my keep."

Kelli watched as Logan stomped down the path without a backward glance. A sudden gust of frigid air blew through the trees. She pulled her legs up on the stump, and wrapped her arms around jean-clad knees. What had happened? One minute he was smiling about still having his two feet and the next he was demanding to cut down trees. One minute he looked ready to kiss her and the next he looked as though she had sprouted two heads.

For one insane moment she wondered what Logan's kiss would have felt like. She shook her head and laughed. Her imagination really must be working overtime. She must have misread the emotion that flared in his brown eyes. It probably was indigestion.

Kelli slowly stood up and for a moment stared down the same path Logan had taken. Then she quickly turned and headed in the opposite direction. She jammed her cold hands into the pockets of her jacket, quickened her pace, and muttered one word, "Distance." Logan would be returning to a foreign desert filled with black gold soon, and her life would settle back into its normal hectic pace. They were enemies. Both wanted something the other had, and there could only be one winner. Ruth and Henry were hers. She'd won them when their family had forfeited them. Logan didn't scare her one bit.

She refused to listen to the soft voice whispering in her ear, *Why are you headed in the opposite direction if he doesn't scare you?*

Logan pushed the peas around the mound of mashed potatoes and lined them up against the pork chop sitting on his plate. He scowled. "Isn't she going to join us for dinner?" he asked Ruth.

Ruth hid her smile as she looked from Kelli's empty chair to Logan's untouched dinner. "She's painting in the shop. She told me to wrap her plate and she would heat it up later."

"Does she skip dinner often?"

Henry leaned back in his chair and studied his nephew. Amusement glistened in his eyes. Ruth might be right about Logan and Kelli. "Can't say that she ever has before."

With a frustrated sigh Logan pushed his plate away. Kelli had been avoiding him since that morning. It was no wonder; he'd practically snapped her head off. Twice he'd gone looking for her to apologize, only to come up empty-handed. This time he'd face her in her lair, say his piece and hopefully she would come for dinner. He handed Ruth his full plate. "Could you please wrap this and put it with Kelli's. We'll be back later for it."

After Logan left, Henry waited by the door, chuckling. "By all the saints, I think you're right, Ruth. I've never seen Logan so upset over nothing."

A smile touched Ruth's wrinkled face and a blush of excitement tinted her cheeks. "Wouldn't it be wonderful if they fell in love? Then we could live here with Logan and Kelli."

Henry reached out with his large hand and gently covered her smaller blue-lined one. "Don't get your hopes up, love. Let nature run its course."

"You're right." She sighed wistfully. "But wouldn't they have the most beautiful babies you ever saw?"

Henry's chuckle sounded across the room as the pet door swung open and a blast of cold air whipped across the linoleum floor. "I guess one of the cats just went out?" he said.

Ruth's brow wrinkled into confusion. "That's funny. I could have sworn all the cats were already out."

Logan glared at the warped door and wondered how to begin this conversation. With more determination than finesse, he threw open the door and announced, "We have to talk."

Kelli dipped the brush into a delicate shade of pink and painted a whimsical smile on the statue in front of her. Tinkerbell's sudden movement caught her attention. There was only one person who caused Tinkerbell to smile like that—Logan. So he'd finally caught up with her. She knew he had been looking for her earlier, but she had purposely avoided him. She wasn't sure why; she put it down to self-preservation.

Reluctantly she slowly lowered the blaring earphones of her Walkman and turned toward her intruder. "Logan?"

He noticed she wore the same paint-smeared sweatshirts and gloves as the day before. The kerosene heater was on full blast, attempting to combat the drafts.

"You didn't come in for dinner."

"I wasn't hungry. I told Ruth that I'd be in later."

"She told me." He closed the door behind him. The only lantern was above her worktable, and he stayed in the shadows. "Why are you avoiding me?" he asked, studying her.

She watched the darkened figure, and masked the sudden anger that shot through her. How dare he come into her home and threaten to take the one thing she held dear and then accuse *her* of avoiding *him*? She calmed herself, drawing from a lesson she'd learned years ago in various foster homes. *When confronted with a force more powerful than yourself, do the complete opposite of what is expected. It confuses the enemy.* "Why would I be avoiding you? I have a lot of painting that has to be done before the park opens. Why don't you pull up a crate and we could have a nice talk while I work?"

Logan watched as she turned around and began to paint a blush onto a fairy. With a shrug he reached for an empty crate that he thought might hold his weight. He dragged it nearer to the heater and closer to Kelli. After several moments of silence he asked, "Did you major in painting at school?"

Kelli finished the fairy's eyelashes before answering. "I was in the art club during high school. I only had a year and a half at a local community college."

"That's when Ben died, wasn't it?"

She stared at the man sitting less than three feet away from her. "Have you been checking up on me?"

"No, just listening to Ruth and Henry sing your praises."

"Ah, and that bothers you?" A knowing smile touched her lips.

"Immensely."

"Why?"

"Because I came here determined to rescue my aunt and uncle, only to discover they don't need rescuing. They are perfectly happy here. I haven't seen any signs of overwork or neglect. In fact I have to say you have gone out of your way to make a home for them."

"Thank you."

"Don't thank me yet." He decided to change the subject. "I want to know who cleaned the living room last night."

With a grimace Kelli quickly dabbed at the grotesque smirk she had given the fairy. She concentrated on the mistake as she asked, "Who cleaned what?"

"The living room. Sometime between last night and this morning it magically cleaned itself."

She turned and faced him. "Don't be silly, Logan. Living rooms don't automatically straighten themselves."

Frustration caused his voice to grow louder. "I know that. Ruth claims she didn't clean it. Did you?"

"Why would I clean the room? It would hurt Ruth's feelings if I went around doing her job."

"If you didn't do it, who did?"

Kelli turned her attention back to the unfinished fairy, hiding her smile. She hadn't actually lied to Logan, just twisted the truth. "Are you sure someone cleaned the room?"

"Yes." After a moment's hesitation he added, "At least I think so. There were newspapers piled on the coffee table."

"And someone moved them?"

"Yes."

A gentle smile curved her lips as she faced Logan again. "I'm sorry, Logan, but moving a pile of newspapers doesn't constitute a cleaning. I'm sure Ruth must have moved the newspapers. She probably never connected that with cleaning the room." She watched him frown and asked, "Was anything else done?"

"Well, maybe dusting."

A small chuckle escaped her throat. "How do you maybe dust?"

Logan ran a hand over his jaw. She was right. He couldn't explain exactly what was done, just that the room looked cleaner. No furniture had been moved, the doorknobs still lined the cabinet in the same order, and the wood basket was stacked as high as ever. Just a pile of newspapers had been moved. "Forget it. I must still be suffering from jet lag."

Kelli clamped her lower lip between her teeth to keep from laughing. "No problem."

"Can I ask a personal question?"

"Sure," she said, wearily, "but that doesn't mean I have to answer."

"Fair enough. Why do you collect doorknobs?"

She laughed out loud. "I wasn't expecting that question."

"What question were you expecting?"

"I'm not sure." A wistful smile touched her mouth. "A lot of people collect keys; they can unlock a pleasant surprise, or lock in something evil. Doorknobs hold the same power. All it takes is a twist of your wrist and, presto, you've opened a door to the other side. Master craftsmen have been making doorknobs for centuries. Today's doorknobs hold no creativity. They're all run off the same press—some are chrome and some are brass, but they are all the same. Years ago people cared about details. Doorknobs are just another small detail that slipped through the system."

"I've noticed that no two doorknobs in your house are the same."

"No two rooms in the house are the same, so why should the doorknobs be?"

He chuckled. "Point taken."

When she bent her head and outlined the dark seductive eyes of a water nymph, he noticed how really beautiful the painter was. Intelligence and health sparkled in her eyes and her cheeks held a rosy glow. Her straight white teeth worried her lower lip as she delicately painted sweeping eyebrows on the enchantress cradled on her lap. A sudden urge to taste those lips came over him. He was just rising to his feet when Tinkerbell started to bark frantically.

Kelli turned around and stared at Tinkerbell. The dog was barking at thin air. Nothing was there. "Tinkerbell, stop that."

When the dog continued to howl, she pulled the whistle from under her sweatshirt and gently blew into it. Abruptly Tinkerbell stopped her wailing and walked over and plopped her head into Kelli's lap. "Good doggie."

Bewildered, Logan asked, "What was she barking at?"

"I don't know. Probably a mouse." Lovingly, she petted the animal, silently praising her for her bravery. After a few strokes, Tinkerbell raised her head and looked around the shed. Seeing nothing, she strolled a few feet away and flopped down on the cracked cement and went back to sleep. "I guess we are safe now." There was laughter in Kelli's voice.

Logan stared at her. He wondered *who* was safe. He surely wasn't. He was about to fraternize with the enemy. "Kelli?"

The paintbrush in Kelli's hand started to tremble as she read the desire in his eyes. His soft brown eyes were demanding a response, some mutual understanding of the emotion being transmitted between them. His hands were gentle as he reached out and removed the heavy water nymph from her lap and placed it on the worktable. "I'm going to kiss you."

"Why?" she asked breathily. "You don't even like me."

"Liking you has nothing to do with it."

"You thought I belonged in some home for demented fairies."

He smiled sympathetically. "I still do."

"And I should allow you to kiss me after that comment?"

His finger reached out and tenderly outlined her pouting lower lip. "I don't remember asking your permission."

"Why, you . . ." Kelli's voice trailed off as the lantern suddenly went out. In the faint glow of the kerosene heater she stared up at the hanging light. "I guess a draft blew it out," she whispered.

Logan's hand slid behind Kelli's head and brought her closer. "Probably."

Kelli's arms wound around his neck as he

moved closer. When his lips were a mere inch away she mumbled, "I didn't notice any draft."

"Neither did I," Logan said against her waiting lips.

A sigh escaped Kelli's throat as his lips settled firmly against hers. She willingly followed his hands as they tenderly pulled her out of the chair and into his arms.

Logan's heart understood the sweet sigh she purred and went into double time. She had to be feeling the same magic, the same oneness he was.

The feel of Logan's tongue tenderly tracing her lower lip caused heat to spiral from her stomach out to her fingertips and toes. With a low moan she pressed her lips closer against his. She ran her fingers through the silky texture of his hair, as his hard chest cushioned her breasts. His large gentle hands caressed her back and brought her hips against his growing arousal.

The feel of his hardening body brought her out of the sensual spell. What was she doing? How could she be kissing him? He was the enemy, the one man who could bring her world down. Slowly lowering her hands, she placed them against his chest and pushed gently.

Logan groaned as Kelli broke the kiss and placed a few desperately needed inches between them. He now knew what Kelli SantaFe tasted like, the nectar of the gods, sweet, delicious, addictive. She'd responded passionately to his kiss. Would she respond to his every touch like that? he wondered. What would it be like to make love to her?

Kelli stared up into the darkness and wished she could see his features. Was he as affected by one kiss as she was? With a determined shake of her head, she realized it didn't matter how the kiss affected him, it wasn't going to be repeated. With more such kisses she knew she could lose much more than Ruth and Henry, she could lose her heart. Her voice shook as she took a step backward. "That shouldn't have happened."

Silently, he agreed with her, but the words refused to be vocalized. How do you tell the woman you want to make love with that you shouldn't be kissing her? His breathing was starting to become more normal as he reached for the hanging lantern. "I'll relight this while you clean up. I promised Ruth we would be in for dinner soon."

"But I still have a lot of painting to do."

The lantern caught on the first try. As he adjusted the flame he said, "You can do it after dinner."

"This is my house, my business, and my painting. I will eat dinner when I'm good and ready."

Logan smiled at the resentment in her voice. So Miss Polite had a temper after all. He was glad. "Aunt Ruth went to a lot of trouble to fix dinner for you, the least you can do is eat it."

She picked up assorted brushes and dropped them into an old Flintstone jelly glass filled with soapy water. She pulled the two top sweatshirts over her head and dropped them over the chair. Yanking off the gloves, she called to Tinkerbell. "Come on, girl. Din-din time. I've suddenly developed a raging appetite."

Logan stood in the middle of the shed and chuckled as the door slammed behind her and the dog. So the Fairy Queen had a temper—one to match the passion he'd tasted. With a wistful sigh for things that could never be, he turned the lantern and heater down and slowly followed Kelli back to the house.

He found Ruth and Henry quietly playing a game of checkers in the living room while Kelli fed logs into the wood stove. Her face was flushed with heat as she turned from the stove and looked at him. "I'll go warm up our dinner."

"Thanks. I'll go get another pile of wood for later." With a smile he left the room and headed back outside.

Ruth and Henry smiled at each other as Kelli turned toward the kitchen. Without saying a word they picked up the checkers and board and headed for their coats. As they passed through the kitchen, Ruth said, "We're heading home now. There's some rice pudding in the refrigerator for dessert."

Kelli slid two full plates into the warm oven. "Thanks for the dinner Ruth. I'm sorry I didn't come in before."

"Nonsense, child. You can eat anytime you want."

She smiled at the older couple. "Henry, I saw all those trees you marked today. That should keep Josh busy tomorrow afternoon. Thanks."

"Josh is going to have a hard time taking that chain saw away from Logan. He was cutting down trees and limbs like a lumberjack today, and seemed to be enjoying himself."

"I'm sure that he'll be bored by it soon. They probably don't have an abundance of trees in the Sudan."

Henry's smile faded as he studied the young woman in front of him. "You could be right, but I've never known Logan to become bored with anything." He quietly pulled on his coat, reached for Ruth's hand, and the two of them headed out the door. "Good night," they called.

Kelli placed silverware and drinks for two on

the small kitchen table. Henry was right; Logan didn't seem to be the kind of man who became bored easily. So how long would he stay here? There was nothing here for him except Ruth and Henry. When was he scheduled to go back to Sudan and the oil fields?

Logan returned and dumped a pile of logs by the hearth in the living room. She carefully took the hot plates from the oven as he hung up his windbreaker and washed up.

He had barely sat down when Kelli asked, "When are you returning to Sudan?"

He swallowed a mouthful of mashed potatoes. "I'm not sure."

Kelli's fingers trembled as she cut into her pork chop. "Why not?"

"I've got a lot of things to clear up here first."

"Meaning Ruth and Henry?"

Compassion shone in his eyes as he carefully set his fork down on his plate. "I'm sorry, Kelli, but when I leave here they will be going with me. It's the right thing for all of us."

With a sudden movement she stood up and faced her rival. "Possession is nine tenths of the law, and since they live here, they're mine. You can't have them."

In frustrated silence Logan watched as Kelli grabbed her coat and slammed out the door. What could he possibly say that would make her understand? They were his family, and he needed them too.

Four

After Kelli had stormed out, Logan spent a quiet evening alone with only troubled thoughts for company. He knew she was, in a sense, correct. What right did he have to claim his aunt and uncle, when he was never around when they needed him? How could he possibly take care of them when he was on the other side of the world? He could hire someone to stay with them, but they didn't need a babysitter. They needed someone to be there when things became too much for them. They needed someone like Kelli.

He lay awake staring at the ceiling mentally listing his options. He could return to Sudan and leave his aunt and uncle living peacefully with Kelli. But that would be shirking his responsibilities. How could he allow a complete stranger to carry his load? Especially a stranger that was so petite, gorgeous, kissable, and so desirable. Even if she were slightly unhinged. With a groan he remembered how potent she had tasted, one hundred-fifty proof. The taste of her went straight to his head. He muttered a colorful curse, kicked the extra cover off his bed, and silently commanded all fairies to leave his head.

His second option was to move them into another house and pay someone to keep an eye on them. He grimaced in disgust. Not only would that be disrespectful, but downright insulting. After the years of unselfish love they had given him, how could he contemplate being so callous?

The third, and most intriguing alternative, was not to return to Sudan. There was plenty of work for a geologist in the United States. He could get a job, buy a house, and live with Ruth and Henry, or at least have them nearby. When sleep finally claimed him, visions of Texan oil fields and oil shale deposits in Colorado filled his mind.

Kelli stumbled into the kitchen by eight the next morning. But Logan was already gone. Ruth said he had to run into town, so she had given him the shopping list. With a painful smile, Kelli thanked her for her thoughtfulness and prayed Logan wasn't a big spender. The coffers at Fairyland were running alarmingly low, and it was still weeks before they opened and started pulling in some money.

After a quick breakfast she headed out into the unusually warm March morning. She found Henry and a group of high school students at the outdoor theater discussing which split-log benches would need work. "Good morning, Henry. Morning, gang."

A chorus of "Hi, Kelli" 's filled the air.

"I know most of you have already met Henry, but for those who didn't"—she grabbed hold of his wrist and pulled him into the circle of youths—"this is Henry Morrison. He's in charge of all the grounds work. He'll be the one handing out orders."

Kelli ignored Henry's look of astonishment.

During the morning, with diplomacy and skill she passed out orders that seemed to come from Henry, conferred with him on four separate occasions, and generally started the ball rolling. By eleven-thirty she was tired, hungry, and immensely proud of the way Henry's chest was puffed out and how his eyes sparkled whenever one of the kids called him Pop. She was headed home for lunch when she spotted Logan's car parked out front.

Quickly, she changed directions and headed toward the pond and the new mamma. She silently lectured herself for being a coward. After staying up half the night to paint fairies, and trying to think of a solution concerning Henry and Ruth, she was still confused. One thing was resolved; she was determined to keep her distance from Logan. Not only was he a threat to her newly found family, he was hell on her hormones. Every time she closed her eyes she relived the kiss they had shared. Never before had a kiss left such an emotional impression. She had shared some kisses with men in the past, but they had been tame, undemanding, and safe. With Logan she felt anything but safe. There was something primitive in his kiss. Something that called to a special part of her and demanded a response. One that she wasn't sure she was ready to give. Especially to a man who was only here temporarily, a known enemy, and one who freely admitted he thought she was unbalanced.

When she spotted Angus gracefully gliding across the pond, a gentle smile touched her lips. She began to hum a lullaby and slowly made her way to Caer and her nest. By the time she reached the lean-to, Caer had left her eggs and was noisily greeting Kelli. With loving hands she praised the new mother, sat down, and softly sang another song.

Fifteen minutes later her entire rendition was completed and Caer was back to her eggs. As she carefully and slowly made her way to the other side of the pond, Kelli spotted a pair of mallard ducks who undoubtedly would be increasing their population later this spring.

With a tired sigh Kelli sat down on a dry bed of grass. The back of her neck ached and tension flowed from her cramped muscles. She turned her face toward the warm sun. It felt wonderful after a long winter. Without a thought to the crinkling grass and anything it might contain, Kelli locked her hands and behind her head and lay back. She closed her eyes and promised herself just five more minutes of peaceful solitude.

Half an hour later, Logan found her asleep in the grass. With a cautious glance at the swans swimming on the other side of the pond, he placed the wicker picnic basket down and carefully spread out an old blanket. As he unzipped his jacket, he wondered what her reaction to his peace offering would be. He had spent the morning in town picking up various magazines and journals on geology. They didn't hold all the answers he needed, but they contained names and addresses of people who did. Tonight when Kelli disappeared into her workshop, he would start writing letters.

He had spent over an hour in the grocery store piling all his favorite foods into the cart. An eighteen-pound turkey caused his mouth to water for Ruth's stuffing. Thick porterhouse steaks, fresh broccoli, and the ingredients for a chocolate cake were added to the overflowing cart. He had picked up double of everything on Ruth's order and jammed the stuffed bags into the trunk of his rental car. When he reached home his trunk was overflowing.

When he saw the expression on Ruth's face as she looked at her two new huge houseplants he knew the trip was a success. For as long as he could remember, her home had been crammed with plants. But there wasn't one single plant in their cottage. Why? When he hinted for an explanation, she skillfully skirted the issue.

As Ruth alternated between tisking over the amount of food he'd bought, and planning the next week's meals, Logan had packed a wicker basket full of food. When Ruth learned he planned to share the picnic with Kelli, she beamed and fetched an old plaid blanket she had seen in the hall closet. Armed with a basketful of good intentions, he went to find Kelli. As he stepped outside into the sunshine he knew instinctively where she was. With the swans at the pond.

Now, he silently placed the basket in the middle of the blanket and stared at the sleeping woman. Streaks of mud coated her boots and worn jeans hugged her legs. A large baggy red sweater covered her from her neck to the tops of her thighs. Her small firm breasts were amplified by her hands being laced behind her head. Arousal raced through Logan's body. He forced his gaze higher. Her lips were softly parted as if waiting for a lover's kiss, and her golden lashes lay against her pink cheeks. A Sleeping Beauty struck by a fairy's spell.

She was beautiful. *How could a woman be so seductive without even trying?* he wondered.

With a visible shake of his head, he reminded himself he was there to thank her for all she had done. And because he'd disregarded his responsibilities, Kelli was now going to be hurt. The kiss they shared last night had been a mistake. It couldn't be repeated. They might come to some kind of mutual agreement on his aunt and uncle, but never on the desire that burned between them.

With a heavy sigh he sat down and reached into the basket for a bottle of soda. He drank half the bottle before coming up for air. With a frown he stared across the pond at the pair of graceful swans and wondered how he had known exactly where to find Kelli . . .

Kelli woke slowly with the terrifying knowledge she wasn't alone. Cautiously peeking out from behind her lashes, she breathed a sigh of relief when she spotted Logan. The blond highlights in his brown hair gleamed in the afternoon sun and a frown marred his brow as he stared out across the pond.

A blush of embarrassment swept up her cheeks. She hated being caught sleeping. In a hurried movement she rose to a sitting position and yanked at her baggy sweater.

"Good morning, sleepyhead."

"I think that should be 'Good afternoon.' "

He watched her try to hide a yawn behind her hand. "I hope you're hungry."

"Hungry?"

With a lofty wave toward the basket, he announced, "Your lunch is served."

Bewilderment shone in her eyes as she glanced from Logan to the picnic basket. *What was he up to now?*

Logan read the confusion in her sleep-filled gray

eyes and smiled his friendliest smile. "It's a peace offering. No matter what my opinion is, you are part of the family now. I think we should at least get to know each other, and possibly become friends." With a little-boy smile tilting up the corners of his mouth, he said, "Come on. I even packed it myself."

Kelli hesitantly stood up, brushed off her backside, and tried to run her fingers through her tangled mane. "What's in it?"

A twinkle of mischief shone in his eyes. "It's a smorgasbord of American food."

She looked down at her muddy boots with disgust. She undid the zippers and pulled them off before sitting down on the blanket. "Didn't they have American food in Sudan?"

"Sure, but by the time Mahmud finished cooking it, it didn't taste American." Logan flipped up the lid of the hamper and pulled out a soda. "I didn't know what foods you liked, so you are getting all of my favorites. If you don't like something, you don't have to eat it."

Kelli took the cold bottle of soda and read the label. "Your favorite soda is sarsaparilla?"

"Do you know how hard it is to find sarsaparilla in Khartoum?"

A sympathetic smile curved her lips. "I could imagine."

Logan returned her smile as he watched her relax and drink her soda. He leaned over and with a flourish produced two hoagies from the depths of the basket. "Your main course, madam."

Kelli's taste buds stood up and cheered. Here was a man who knew the way to a woman's heart.

Logan watched as she slowly unwrapped her American hoagie, with the works, as if the answers to the universe were held inside the paper. He laughed as a full-blown grin lit up Kelli's face. "What's so funny?"

Kelli smiled at Logan and wondered how to answer. For a horrible moment she thought he was trying to seduce her with food. When she unwrapped the hoagie and spotted the mound of onions nestled between the meat, cheese, lettuce, and tomato, she knew her fears were unfounded. No man brought onions to a woman he was planning to seduce. She picked up the sandwich. "Nothing's funny, I just love hoagies." Then she took a large bite. Satisfied with her answer, he picked up his sandwich and got down to the serious business of lunch.

Kelli wiped juice from the tomato from her chin and groaned. Logan had finished first, but she had put up a good fight. "I concede. When it comes to hoagies, you're a bigger pig than I."

He had watched a small drop of juice roll down her chin and groaned. It would have been so easy to reach over and gently capture the moistness with his mouth. When she wiped the juice away with a paper napkin, frustration ravaged his body. He placed a friendly smile on his face and said, "Sorry. I didn't mean for it to turn into a race."

Kelli finished off the rest of her soda, leaned back on her elbows, and watched Caer waddle toward her nest. "No need to apologize. I never can resist a challenge."

Logan leaned back and faced the pond. The silence that surrounded them was broken only by an occasional honk from the swans, or a gentle chirping from nearby birds. After a few restful minutes he said, "Tell me about Ben."

She sighed wistfully. "He was brilliant. He could

fix or build anything. Do you know he built the house all by himself?"

"Is he the one who installed the doorbell that plays 'We're Off to See the Wizard'?"

"He made me that chime for my seventeenth birthday."

"Impressive. I suppose he also was the inventor of Killer, your attack dog."

She softly chuckled, and said, "Afraid so."

"You miss him, don't you?"

She had to clear the lump that had caught in her throat before she could answer. "Every day."

Logan forced himself to remain seated and not to gather her in his arms and promise her everything would work out. "Did you love him?"

"Like a father. When I first moved in with him there was some serious speculation in town."

"About what?"

"A sixteen-year-old hoodlum and a fifty-year-old man. Youth Services did more than their share of checking up on him. It's really funny, the one person who everyone thought would be bad for me turned out to be the best. People in town didn't understand Ben. He was a loner. He never went into town, unless he had to. The only friend he had was Josh's grandfather. They were fishing buddies."

"That's how you met Josh."

"Yes. When the whispers in town started, Ben and Emmett, Josh's grandfather, had this idea to pair us up. Since Josh didn't have a steady girlfriend, we went along with it."

He studied her profile. "Nothing serious came of it?"

"No, much to Ben's and Emmett's disappointment."

"Why? Josh seems like the all-American dream date."

Kelli laughed merrily. "If you'd seen Josh eight years ago, you wouldn't have said that. Every father in town forbade his daughters from even talking to him."

"Josh?"

"Yep. He rode the biggest Harley-Davidson in the county and wore a gold crucifix in his right ear. His idea of dressing up was clean jeans and polishing his sunglasses."

"And Ben allowed you to date him?"

"We made a perfect pair. I was rebelling against the town for gossiping about me and he was furious at the daughters for listening to their fathers. Wherever we went, people knew we were there."

"But he's a policeman."

"Now he is; then he was just a frustrated young man. We both made the honor roll, and every time we aced a test they yanked us to the office and accused us of cheating." After a thoughtful moment, she asked, "Do you know something, Logan?"

"What?"

"People do judge a book by its cover."

Logan was angry for her sake. Poor Kelli. A frightened teenager thrown to a pack of wolves, only to be torn apart at every change. Being forced to listen to vicious talk about Ben, the one man who loved her enough to pull her off the streets. "I'm sorry."

Kelli heard the disgust in his voice and smiled. "Thanks, but it's been over for six years. I turned respectable the year I started college and Josh left for the police academy. Now boys who use to proposition me with some very interesting ideas bring their kids and wives here to see the fairies."

She chuckled. "Josh is now the town's number-one catch. Every mother is practically throwing their virginal beauties at his feet."

"Ah, but is he biting?"

"To the great disappointment of every mother—and some very testy daughters—he hasn't even nibbled."

He lifted his brow, amazed. "Nothing?" He watched Kelli shake her head and eye the picnic basket. "Interesting."

"No, predictable. Did you bring anything else?"

"Of course." He lifted the lid of the hamper. "Why predictable?"

Her mouth watered as she saw the bag of potato chips. "They're still judging the book by its cover."

"Are you saying he's not true-blue under that badge?"

She narrowed her eyes. "All I'm saying is he's the same today as he was nine years ago. Loyal, honest, and the best friend I ever had."

"I seem to be apologizing to you a lot today. I'm sorry. I won't question your friendship with Josh again." He saw her guarded expression and pulled up a cellophane package of Ding Dongs. "Am I forgiven?"

"Maybe."

"For two chocolate cakes surrounding a heap of delicious cream all covered with dark chocolate, I need a definite answer."

"Yes, providing I get to ask the next question."

He smiled graciously and handed her the package and another sarsaparilla. "Sure. I have all my own teeth, stopped believing in Santa Claus by the time I was ten, and flunked my driver's test the first two times. I'm allergic to asparagus, deplore horror movies, and my favorite color is yellow.

"I love my job, can't spell worth a damn, and my checkbook's never balanced. I've never married, but I once lived with a girl during college. I don't believe in ironing, ESP, or that we will one day balance the national budget. Did any of that answer any of your questions?"

A mischievous smile touched her lips as she shook her head. "No. I was just curious if you always wore such interesting shorts."

Startled, he asked, "My shorts?"

"Yeah, you know, those cute boxers. I especially like the green ones with the light bulbs all over them."

"How in the hell would you know what my shorts look like?"

Her voice was all innocence. "I did the wash this morning."

Logan willed back his embarrassment. He was a thirty-four-year-old man and the subject of his shorts shouldn't cause him to blush like a schoolboy. "I thought Ruth was the housekeeper."

"She is, but I do all the laundry."

"Why?"

"The machine is very temperamental. It only listens to me. The two times she tried to wash a load catastrophe struck."

"Catastrophe?"

"The first time the water hose snapped and we ended up with a flood in the laundry room. The second time it wouldn't rinse the suds out of the clothes."

Logan studied Kelli's serene expression; something wasn't right. A housekeeper who didn't do laundry? A living room that magically cleaned itself? In the two days he had been there, Ruth had baked and cooked meals that Kelli usually wasn't around for. When it was time for the dishes, Henry or Kelli was always there to lend a helping hand. When his aunt had some free time she was either napping or knitting Kelli another red sweater. But he would get to the bottom of the housekeeper who never kept house later; he decided to answer her original question now. "My shorts are a conversation piece."

Kelli looked at Logan's earnest expression and burst out laughing. The more she thought about it, the more she laughed. An image of Logan standing there in just his outrageous skivvies didn't inspire conversation. Lust? Maybe. Wanton desires? Probably. A need for a quiet tête-à-tête? Never! She would be lucky if she could breathe in such a situation. As the laughter subsided she barely choked out, "Do you like to hold conversations while you stand around in your B.V.D.'s?"

He grinned. She had a magical laugh. It held the sweetness of youth, a promise of passion, and the silkiness of seduction. Put it all together and she was arousing him with a laugh. He suddenly shifted position and wondered when he had become a masochist. He suddenly had to hear that laugh again. He held up an imaginary cigar while wiggling his eyebrows in his best Groucho Marx fashion. "Anytime you want, I'll take off my pants and chat up a storm. Just let me know."

She adored his humor. It said a lot about the man. She wasn't sure how she would have handled a friendly chat about her undies, but he was handling it marvelously.

Maybe too marvelously. This afternoon she had fallen for his charm and had completely forgotten about being enemies. Distrust and sadness replaced the laughter in her eyes. No sense crying for the moon. As a child she had learned that wishing for unattainable things only made the pain linger. With a sigh of regret she brought their camaraderie to an end. "When are you going back?"

Logan knew the instant the harmony between them broke. It was written in her eyes. He ran a frustrated hand through his hair and groaned. "I told you last night, I don't know."

"The company you work for just told you to take as much time as you like? Come back when you're ready?"

"It's more complicated than that. My contract was up. Now I can either renegotiate and return to Khartoum or some other overseas field, or I can find another job."

Panic ripped through her. If he didn't return overseas, that meant he would either be moving away, taking her family with him . . . or becoming a permanent guest at Fairyland. Either way spelled disaster. She tried to keep her voice steady. "What do you *want* to do?"

"I'm checking into some matters before I make a final decision."

Kelli's mind screamed for her to think, and fast. "There must be a lot of benefits that come with staying with one company ten years. Pensions, insurance, K-plans, not to mention the travel. I'm sure all that will play a key role in your decision."

"Kelli, I know all the pros and cons. My main concern right now is for my aunt and uncle. What's best for them."

"Why not just ask them?"

Logan collapsed onto his back and stared up at the fluffy clouds in the sky. How could he explain the atmosphere that surrounded Fairyland? It was beautiful, serene, and enchanted. A place where magical beings roamed. Ruth and Henry had a modest and comfortable home, everything they could need and a sense of being wanted. Why would they leave? But was it the right place for them? "They're my responsibility."

"They're old enough to make their own decisions," snapped Kelli.

"Listen, I'm trying to do what's best for them."

"Best for *whom*?" she asked pointedly.

Aggravated by the sudden change in her mood, he growled, "They are my family. I will work out something."

Hurt, anger, and fear tightened her chest. She tried to hold back her tears. "Am I supposed to sit back and let you take them away from me?"

He watched her fighting back her sadness, and cursed. He had hurt her. In a swift movement he sat up and knelt beside her. He tenderly placed his hands on her shoulders and gently squeezed. "We'll work something out."

Kelli looked into his honest, pleading eyes and believed him. A tentative smile touched her lips. "Have any suggestions?"

"Visitation rights."

"Visitation rights! Are you out of your mind? Are you suggesting we alternate weekends with them?" When he just continued to stare at her, she continued, "What about Christmas? Would you get them Christmas Eve, and allow me Christmas morning? Have you given any thought to birthdays and their anniversary? Are you out of your mind?"

He tried to smile. "You've already asked me that."

Flabbergasted, she said, "You *are* out of your mind. Do you realize we are talking about your aunt and uncle? This is your family. I know parents shuffle their kids between each other, but I've never heard of grandparent custody." Drawing in a deep breath, she glared at the grin spreading across his face. "Wipe that silly smirk off your face, you idiot. You can't possibly be serious about this. It must have been the sun. Ten years in the Middle East must have fried your brains. No sane man would make such an asinine suggestion."

"Kelli?"

"What?"

"Shut up." Gently pulling her pouting mouth closer, he said, "Lord, you're beautiful when you get riled."

A soft "oh" escaped her parted lips before his seized them.

Five

Kelli felt the warm gentle pressure of his lips and every thought vanished from her mind. Her arms reached around his neck and with a groan drew him nearer.

Logan heard the sweet sound she made, and was lost. His tongue plunged past her lips as he lovingly lowered her back onto the blanket. Heat coiled low in his body as his chest brushed against her breasts. He broke the kiss and trailed a heated path of kisses down her throat. When he came to the barrier of her sweater he slowly lifted his head and gazed down into her darkened eyes. He had had women before, but Kelli was different. The others had been mutual wanting, this was a desperate need. Resting his weight on his elbows he tenderly cupped her face. "Are you real?" He saw confusion cloud her eyes. "Sometimes I think you're a fairy and will disappear in a puff of smoke if I touch you."

Kelli tried to catch her breath as she gazed up at him. "Why?"

His hand brushed a wisp of hair off her flushed

face. "I think you've cast a spell over me. I've never felt like this before. I want you, but I can't have you. When I leave here, I'm going to hurt you enough by taking my aunt and uncle. I don't want to hurt you more by throwing in other emotions."

Kelli closed her eyes, trying to block the pain his words caused. He was taking her family and he didn't want any emotions to get in the way. Fine! She could play by those rules. When she reopened her eyes, a glint of anger shone in her gaze. "Are you finished?"

He stopped caressing her lower lip with his thumb, and nodded.

"Then do you mind letting me up? I've got a park to get ready for its opening."

Logan felt her anger and quickly rolled off her. He frowned as she stood up and casually smoothed her sweater down. She bent over, pulled her muddy boots back on, and ran her fingers through her hair. "Thanks for the lunch, Logan. It was interesting."

He sat transfixed for a silent minute as she turned and started to walk away. "Is that all you're going to say?" he asked, incredulous.

Without breaking her stride, she turned and said, "No. You're a horse's patoot."

Logan sat and watched as she faded into the woods. She was right; he was a horse's patoot. Not because he believed he was the one responsible for Ruth and Henry, but because he was letting her walk away.

Half an hour later he found Henry surrounded by a group of adoring teenagers who were following his every command. "What's up, Uncle Henry?"

"Hello, son, I was wondering when you'd show

up." He gestured toward the group of youths. "This is the drama club Kelli's always talking about. They came here to clean up the theater area. The tech school is sending over the carpentry class Monday morning to start work on some of these benches and to make some minor repairs to the stage."

Logan glanced around the area and counted at least twelve kids and one other adult. No Kelli. The older gentleman walked up to him, stuck out his hand, and said, "Hi, you must be Logan. I'm Dan Teeterman, the head of the drama club."

The men shook hands. "Logan Sinclair. You seem to have everything under control. Do you need any help?"

"Not right now. Josh just took down a humdinger of a tree for us."

"Josh is here?"

"He and Kelli just left for the creek. There seems to be a jam somewhere."

"Well, since you can't use me," said Logan, "I think I'll go lend Josh a hand." With a general farewell to everyone he headed in the direction of the creek.

He heard them before he actually saw them. Josh's booming voice came from ahead. "Get your butt over here, woman."

"I don't think I have these on right," Kelli replied. "They're bagging around the thighs."

Logan stopped in his tracks. What was going on? Unsure if he should round the last clump of bushes, he listened as Josh bellowed, "That's because you've got skinny legs. Now get over here, I need you, now!"

He had heard enough. The way Josh was shouting, Logan didn't want Kelli anywhere near him. With three powerful strides, he passed the last obstacle and blinked at the sight greeting him. Josh was thigh-deep in the middle of the creek, holding on to a massive log. Kelli was timidly stepping into the stream, cursing. She was wearing thigh-high fisherman boots held by thick black suspenders.

From the look on Josh's face, he was about to lose his grip on the log and his patience. "Damn, woman, move it. I know this isn't your favorite pastime, but it is your creek and your jam."

Kelli slowly inched her way into the deeper water. "Are you sure there're no snakes?"

A colorful curse exploded in the air. "Kelli, the water still has ice in it. I have never heard of polar snakes. So get your tush over here and help me get this log out of *your* creek before it breaks free and does some major damage."

Kelli felt her feet sink deeper into the soft bottom of the creek and grimaced. She forced herself to grab hold of the freezing log, determined to overcome her fear of snakes. She smiled hesitantly. "Now what?"

"On the count of three, we'll *slowly* push it toward the bank. One, two . . ."

Kelli spotted a sinister movement across the surface of the creek. "Snake!" she screamed. Panic stricken she turned toward the bank. But her feet were stuck in mud and the sudden movement threw her off balance. She tipped backward with a large splash.

Josh made a grab for Kelli, and lost his grip on the log. The wood broke free of its mooring and crashed into his chest. He went under with a thud just as Kelli came up sputtering water and choking.

Logan reached the bank in four huge steps and dove into the shallow stream. He reached Kelli the same instant Josh's head emerged from the freezing grimy water. With more force than finesse Logan quickly whacked Kelli on her back.

The force of his slap nearly sent her under the icy water again. She cleared her throat and choked, "Logan, I'm okay."

Josh had recovered quickly. He was already smiling. But Kelli still looked shaken. As Kelli regained her breath, Logan gently tried to lift her into his arms. He cursed as he realized her hip boots were weighing her down. He held her with one arm as he worked the suspenders off her shoulders.

"Logan, put me down."

Her body was still trembling, and the way she bravely tried to smile tore at his heart. His arms tightened their hold. "No," he said. He looked over at Josh. The other man was shaking frigid water from his hair. "Are you okay?"

Josh brushed at a clump of brown weeds stuck to his soaking flannel shirt and groaned. "Sure, I'm fine." He glared at Kelli and said, "I feel like I was just run over by a truck while being forced to drink five gallons of swamp water."

Kelli reached over Logan's shoulder and tenderly brushed at Josh's dripping hair. "I'm sorry, Josh. I thought I saw a snake."

"I know. I heard your scream." He shook his head smiling, his good humor intact.

"Let's get Kelli home," Josh said.

Kelli glared up at the man carrying her. "Put me down, Logan," she demanded. "I am perfectly capable of walking."

Without a downward glance, Logan said, "Shhhh. Your body had just received a shock." A mischievous gleam shone in his eyes. "Even with the weight of your wet clothes, I guess I can manage to carry you back to the house."

Kelli gave Josh a deadly glare when he laughed.

Logan had taken two steps toward the bank when a frantically barking Tinkerbell dashed from the woods and flew down the embankment. With a huge spray of water, Tinkerbell headed right for Kelli. Logan took a protective step backward as Josh tackled the distraught dog. While Josh wrestled Tinkerbell, Logan safely made it to the bank with his precious burden.

Kelli craned her neck and shouted, "Down, girl." She watched as Josh fell backward into the stream again. When his head reemerged she reached for the dog whistle around her neck and softly blew. Tinkerbell was obedient immediately. "Come, girl."

Josh spit out another mouthful of foul water and glared at the dog. With a powerful yank he pulled Kelli's boots free of the mud, drained the water from them, and carried them to the bank. While Logan waited impatiently, Josh tugged off his own water-filled boots, and joined them for the long, cold walk back to the house.

"Why is she scared to death of snakes? And why in the hell was she in the water to begin with?"

Kelli stiffened in his arms. "*She* can answer for herself. You don't have to talk like I'm not here. I'm not scared to death of snakes, I just don't like them."

"Why were you in the water then?" he asked.

"Josh needed someone to help him."

"Why didn't you ask me?"

"This is *my* property. I've been clearing that creek for years before you showed up, and I'll be doing it for years after you're gone."

Logan stopped and stared down at the woman

in his arms. "You're a stubborn, pigheaded fool. Do you have any idea what that log could of done to you, if it hit you instead of Josh?"

Kelli's chin rose and managed to stare down her nose at Logan. "It didn't. You can put me down, now."

Logan muttered an oath. "I should put you down. Right back where I found you, in the middle of the creek."

She shot a murderous glare at Josh, who was laughing. "What do *you* think is so funny?"

Josh couldn't appear serious. "You two," he said, chuckling.

They had almost reached the house when Logan suddenly demanded, "Why in the hell did you allow her to help you?"

"How in the blazes did you expect me to stop her?" Josh replied indignantly. "When she makes up her mind, it's final. There's no way I, or anyone else, could have stopped her."

Logan suddenly smiled. "I could have," he said.

Josh studied Logan and the woman snuggled in his arms. "I believe you could have," he said quietly.

Kelli groaned as the house came into sight. "Will you two stop playing cave man and put me down!"

When Logan threw open the kitchen door and rushed across the room Ruth dropped a mixing bowl. "Bring up a bottle of brandy and two glasses," he said.

"Don't listen to him, Ruth," Kelli pleaded.

"We don't have any brandy." Ruth sounded concerned.

Logan stopped at the opening into the living room and asked, "What kind of liquor is in the house?"

"Just a couple of beers that are Josh's."

Kelli rolled her eyes and glared at the ceiling. "Is anyone listening to me. I don't want a drink. I don't need a drink. All I want is to be put down."

"Fix some hot cocoa with plenty of sugar and bring it up to the bathroom," he shouted over his shoulder as he dashed upstairs with Kelli clutched in his arms. "And help Josh find some dry clothes."

Logan reached into the shower and turned on the hot water. He adjusted the spray, and stepped under the spray with her still in his arms.

As the heat warmed their skin, he said gently, "Isn't this better then a freezing creek?"

Kelli felt the warm water pour over her, and sighed. "Heaven." She closed her eyes and pressed closer to him. Maybe if she stayed here for a month the feeling in her fingers would return. She was grateful when he pulled the sweater over her head to allow the heat of the water to beat against her bare shoulders. She kept her eyes closed and relished in the feeling of Logan's touch combined with the hot spray.

Logan gently undressed her down to her jeans and a pale pink camisole. He quickly shed his own clothes, except for a pair of boxer shorts with lollipops. As Logan rinsed the mud off them, he flung the muddy clothes into the sink along with their shoes. When the water started to run clear he set the stopper and let the tub fill. By the time the water was ankle deep he had Kelli sitting next to him. Kelli was laughing.

He breathed a sigh of relief. For awhile there he thought she really might be going into shock. She hadn't said a word the whole time he had undressed her. "Feeling warmer?"

The sight of Logan in his sexy skivvies doing a

great impression of a pretzel brought a chuckle. She could feel her camisole plastered to her chest and the weight of her wet jeans pressed uncomfortably against her legs. "Yes, thank you."

"You're welcome."

She had trouble finding a safe place to rest her hands in the small confines of the tub. "So this is what it's like to shower with a man."

Logan swallowed at the implication behind her statement. She'd never showered with a man before. In a playful tone he said, "You were expecting tug boat races?"

Just then the door opened. Logan looked up as Josh, dressed in borrowed sweats, walked in carrying a tray with two cups of hot cocoa and a thermos. He was silent, but his eyes were wide.

"Kelli, quick tell Josh I'm behaving," Logan said.

Kelli looked over her shoulder at her friend and softly smiled. "He's right, Josh. He's behaving like a perfect gentleman."

"He's in his underwear," roared Josh.

She gave Logan an amused glance. "I've seen men wear less at the beach, and besides they're a conversation piece."

Josh stood there for several seconds holding the tray. He had been concerned about her, when all the time she was frolicking with a partially clad man in her bathtub. The color was back in her cheeks, and her jeans were on, so he guessed he'd let Logan live. "I'll just leave this here," he said, as he placed the tray on the toilet lid. "I'll tell Ruth you both are fine, and will be down in a few minutes."

"Thanks, Josh," Logan and Kelli said in unison.

"You're welcome. I'll see you in a couple of

minutes." As Josh left, he purposely left the door open a few inches.

"I don't think he likes me," Logan said, as he handed a steaming cup to Kelli. He had noticed that the door was ajar, but that was fine with him. He wasn't planning a big seduction scene. The shower was for purely medical purposes.

"He's acting like my older brother again. He does that quite a lot."

Logan watched as she took a hesitant sip of cocoa and licked the foam off her lips. The pink camisole she wore was soaking wet, transparent, and clinging to her breasts. Her dusky nipples were clearly outlined and the heat in the bathroom seemed to be rising. "Hasn't he ever seen you take a bath with a man before?" he joked, trying to relieve the tension he felt.

With a saucy grin, Kelli finished her cocoa and studied the man next to her. He was now turned sideways with his feet dangling out of the tub. His hair was slicked back and a nonchalant smile curved his lips as he drank. A light feathering of hair covered his chest and legs, his ridiculous shorts covered the essentials.

Logan felt her curious glance and forced himself to relax. When her eyes locked in on his lollipops, he shifted position and reached for the thermos. "Do you want another?"

Kelli held out her cup for a refill. "Thanks." She took a sip of the hot liquid and placed her cup on the edge of the tub. "I want to thank you for being there today. I'm not sure how you got there, but thanks."

"You're welcome." Logan gently lifted her chin and placed a tender kiss on her surprised mouth. "Sometimes a person needs help. It doesn't make them weaker, just more human."

"Logan, I do ask for help when I need it. Going into the creek to help Josh was something I had to do."

"Why?"

"I wouldn't let some childish fear of a legless lizard get the best of me."

"You are the most stubborn woman I've ever met." His anger slowly faded as he gazed at a single drop of water that was slowly trailing down her cheek. It hung on the edge of her delicate jaw, before gathering strength and rapidly descending her throat, only to disappear in her softly rounded cleavage.

She backed away from the intense look in his eyes. "Why don't I go wait in the hall while you finish taking a proper shower?"

A gentleman would have insisted that she go first. But a gentleman wouldn't be in his condition. "Sounds great to me."

She stood up, allowing the water to run off her jeans and drip on the floor. Just then, an ungodly ruckus broke out in the hall. Ruth shrieked; Henry yelled; Tinkerbell barked; and it sounded suspiciously like Josh was laughing. Kelli looked with horror at the door. She knew what was about to happen, but she was powerless to stop it.

Tinkerbell burst through the door and in one flying leap landed in the tub. Kelli lost her balance and landed on top of him with a splash. Tinkerbell's pink tongue lovingly licked the water from Kelli's resigned face as she tried to sit up again.

Logan took a deep breath. There was no way he would ever be able to father a child. No way. Gingerly he lifted Tinkerbell's rear paw from a very sensitive area. He forced a carefree smile, noticing the curious group of onlookers standing in the doorway. With a push he removed the muddy, hairy rump from in front of his nose. "Life doesn't get any better than this," he said.

When Kelli was clean and dry, she descended the steps just as Ruth announced, "I'm going to scrub the floor."

Kelli sneezed loudly and dramatically and walked sluggishly into the kitchen. "I think I've caught a cold."

Ruth's reaction was exactly as Kelli expected. With a quickness that was surprising for her age, Ruth replaced the bucket and scrub brush and rushed to Kelli. Her wrinkled hands caressed Kelli's cheeks and she pressed against her forehead. "You don't feel hot, but you do look peaked."

Kelli hid her grimace. It was one thing to be sick and look peaked, but it was entirely different to be healthy and have someone say you look like hell. In a little girl's voice, guaranteed to win over grandmothers, she asked, "Do we have any soup?"

Ruth helped Kelli to a chair. "You sit right down. I'll fix you a nice cup of tea with honey. Then I'll work on dinner."

"Thanks," Kelli murmured softly. Then she glanced at the three men sitting at the table. Henry looked relieved, Josh was amused, and Logan looked angry. "Henry, did the kids go home?" Kelli asked.

"Yes, they said they'll be back next weekend."

"Great. Josh, what about the log? How much damage did it do?"

Josh was dressed in a pair of Logan's sweats now, but his hair was still damp. "None. It jammed about ten feet from where we lost it. Logan and I went back out to check. It's solid. We are going to wait until the boots dry out before *we* remove it."

Ruth placed a cup of steaming tea in front of Kelli and gave the men a reproachful glare. "No more business today. Can't you see that Kelli isn't feeling well?" She smiled a motherly smile as she handed Kelli a jar of honey. "Now you drink this up and then go lie down on the sofa for a while. I'll wake you when dinner's ready."

As Kelli sipped her tea Josh made a speedy exit, saying he didn't want to catch any germs. Henry agreed to help Ruth chop up vegetables. Logan continued to glare at her.

After placing her empty cup on the counter, she went into the living room, curled up on the worn couch, and closed her eyes.

The room was dark, except for the glow from the wood stove. Silently, Kelli studied the man squatting in front of the stove. Logan was bathed in the illuminating firelight and he quietly fed a log to the flames. His light brown hair gleamed and the deep tan of his skin shone in the heat. His faded jeans stretched across his thighs as he balanced on the balls of his feet. He was beautiful. A man who could laugh at himself, dive into a creek to save a damsel in distress, and also hold the power to break her heart.

Logan heard Kelli sigh softly. He turned around. "I always seem to be around when you're waking up."

She kicked off the afghan covering her. "Is that a nice way of saying I sleep too much?"

He placed the last log into the stove and closed its door. The room was plunged into darkness.

"No, on the contrary, I think you don't sleep enough."

"Some days I would have to agree with you. What time is it?"

"Time to eat the soup Aunt Ruth made especially for you. It's simmering on the back burner of the stove."

Kelli noticed the sarcastic note in his voice as he walked into the kitchen. He was right to be a bit miffed. She had tricked Ruth into making the soup—but Kelli had her reasons. Tomorrow she would have another talk with Ruth. It was time to tell Logan the truth, only it wasn't her story to tell.

Logan sat up in bed, alert. Something had awakened him. Voices. *Burglars?* He never had liked Kelli leaving the doors unlocked. He slipped from under the blankets and reached for his jeans. Almost as an afterthought he pulled on socks and a sweatshirt. Hell, if he had to chase a crook at three in the morning, he wanted to be dressed for it.

He quietly opened his bedroom door and glanced down the stairs. Nothing. The living room was dark. A small night-light burned at the top of the steps showing Kelli's door was closed and the bathroom unoccupied. More annoyed than fearful he made his way down the stairs, across the living room, and toward the kitchen.

He pressed his ear against the closed door. Not voices; *a* voice. Kelli's voice to be precise. He quietly cracked the door and peered in. The sight that greeted him surprised, amused, and confused him. All four chairs were stacked on the kitchen table, along with the throw rugs. Cobweb was on top of the refrigerator, Mustardseed was curled up under the chairs, and Moth was playing with Kelli's toes. Kelli knelt in the middle of the floor scrubbing the linoleum. She was lecturing the cats on the subject of men.

"Men, who in the blue blazes needs them," she told them. "I was doing perfectly fine here alone. Then he marches in here and starts judging me! I'm doing him a favor, but do I get any thanks? No! I have to sit through dinner listening to him expound about how much work Ruth put into making the soup, just for me."

She pointed the scrub brush at Cobweb. "Was there anything else I could have done? No. I did the only thing I could think of at the spur of the moment, and not one word of thanks. That's a man for you. I'm telling you, Cobweb, if you know what's good for you, stay away from Moth. He's no good for you. He goes out carousing for days at a time. His markings are on half the cats in this county and all he has to do is bat those emerald-green eyes and you're a goner." She moved to attack another stretch of floor, dragging Moth, who was hanging on to her sock, behind her. "It's disgusting the power they have just because of a lazy strut and a flashy tail."

Logan cleared his throat. "My, my, what have we here? Could this be a magical fairy doing the mysterious cleaning?"

Kelli jerked around, spilling half the bucket of soapy water on the floor. With a colorful oath she quickly started to sop up the excess liquid. She cast a vicious glance over her shoulder. "If you ever scare me again like that, I'll—"

"Yes?"

She wrang out the rag again, and snapped, "I'll starch every pair of skivvies you own."

He managed to keep a straight face. "I'll take heed of your threat and try to be careful in the future." When she didn't smile, he asked, "What are you doing?"

She scrubbed at a grease mark. "What does it look like?"

"Scrubbing the floor."

She glanced sarcastically at Mustardseed. "Give the man a blue ribbon. You can tell he didn't fall off a turnip truck."

Logan came into the room and squatted beside her. Her hair was pulled back into a ponytail with a red band, and she wore a baggy red sweatshirt. "You're upset about something," he said.

She continued to scrub a wide path in the linoleum. "I get like this when I'm forced to eat dinner and guilt at the same time."

He moved back, out of her reach. "Mind explaining?"

Kelli knew the time had come, was past due in fact. He had the right to know about Ruth. Except it wasn't her business to tell him. Ruth had kept the secret from him for eight years. Now was the time to pay the piper. With a frustrated gesture, she dropped the brush into the bucket and looked at Logan. "I'm sorry, I can't. I promise you, by Monday morning you will have your answer."

"Monday?" She nodded. "Are you going to tell me?"

In a serious tone she said, "If need be."

Logan looked around the kitchen and noticed the gleam to the cabinet doors and the sparkle to the counter. Kelli had been one busy woman tonight. He read fatigue and honesty in her large gray eyes. He could wait until Monday. "Okay. No more questions till then."

"Thanks."

"If you have another bucket, I'll get the mud I tracked through the living room and up the stairs."

Kelli finally smiled. She rose gracefully, picked up Moth, and filled another bucket with hot water and cleaner. She was tired and wanted to go to bed. It had been a hard day. Before she'd come downstairs to clean, she had sat at the desk in her bedroom trying to balance Fairyland's books. Balancing the national budget would have been easier.

She handed Logan the bucket. "There's one condition. Tomorrow morning, don't mention this little episode."

"My lips are sealed until Monday." As he headed out of the kitchen he said to himself, "Only till Monday."

Six

Logan glanced at the slip of paper Kelli had given
him and reread the address. He was at the right
place. Sweat broke out on his brow. The brass
plate affixed to the front door of the grand Victo-
rian building read JAMES B. YOUNG, M.D.—SPECIALIST
IN CARDIOVASCULAR DISEASES. With a sense of dread
he pushed open the door and entered the waiting
room.

When the door opened, Kelli looked up from a
magazine. Logan was on time. He paused at the
door, uncertain, until he spotted her. She admired
the picture he created as he walked across the
room. He looked sporty and casual. But when he
reached her, she saw the anxiety on his face. She
tried to reassure him with a smile.

She placed the magazine back on the end table,
and gently took his hand. "They're expecting us."

Logan felt the warmth of Kelli's fingers entwine
with his cold hand as he followed her to the receptionist's desk. In a low voice he asked, "Who's
expecting us, and why?"

Kelli gave his hand an encouraging squeeze as

the receptionist looked up and smiled. "You must be Ruth's nephew, Logan Sinclair. Kelli has already explained everything to us. If you would just follow me, I'm sure your aunt and Dr. Young will be along shortly."

Logan felt Kelli try to pull away, and he gripped her hand tighter. He followed the receptionist down the hall, dragging Kelli behind him.

When he and Kelli were alone in the doctor's private office, Logan snapped at her. "What in the hell is going on? Is there something wrong with Aunt Ruth? Where is she? Why wasn't I told until now?" He dragged his free hand through his hair and glared at her. "Say something, dammit."

Kelli fought the guilty flush sweeping up her cheeks. He had every right to be upset. If the situation was reversed, she'd be demanding answers too. "Please, Logan, you're hurting my hand."

Logan instantly released her hand. His "sorry" was drowned out by the entrance of Ruth and the doctor.

Ruth became distressed when she spotted Logan standing in the middle of her doctor's office.

"I'm sorry, Ruth," said Kelli, "but you have to tell him. He has a right to know." She saw tears pool behind Ruth's thick glasses and gently kissed her cheek. "Dr. Young will be here to answer Logan's questions, so you won't have to go into detail."

Ruth released Kelli's hands. "Where are you going?"

"I'll be in the waiting room. There's a magazine with a really interesting article on the breast-feeding of the woolly spider monkey."

A tentative smile curved Ruth's mouth as she watched Kelli beat a hasty exit, closing the door behind her. Ruth squared her shoulders and faced her nephew. "She really knows how to make an exit," she said.

Kelli had glanced through five magazines and bitten three fingernails down to the skin by the time she heard Logan's deep voice in the hall. When she saw Ruth's beaming face, Kelli released the breath she'd been holding and hurried toward her. "Everything's okay?"

"Wonderful, child." Ruth gave Logan an affectionate glance. "He took it quite well. In fact, I'm relieved he finally knows." Ruth kissed Kelli's cheek.

"I told you so," Kelli whispered. She watched Logan confer with the receptionist. Charts and payment schedules were being pulled from folders and spread over the desk.

Logan frowned at the growing mound of paperwork. For eight years the amount that Medicare didn't cover on each visit had accumulated into a substantial debt. He picked up the latest record and studied it. Not only had someone paid the small amount for each visit for the last six months, but they were trying to hack away at the larger chunk. He raised an eyebrow. He glanced over at Kelli, the only thing that had changed in Ruth's life in the past six months. She was standing next to his aunt, grinning. She was dressed in black stretch pants and a trademark oversized red sweater with a black question mark knitted into the front. White sneakers with red polka-dotted shoelaces completed her outfit. Her red beaded earrings swung against her neck as she turned and reached for Ruth's coat.

"Why don't you two wait for me out front," said Logan.

Kelli held the coat as Ruth slipped her arms into the sleeves. She hesitated. She really should settle the bill with the doctor, she knew, but since Logan had a death grip on it, she'd wait until next month. "Sure," she said.

Logan waited until the door closed behind them. The receptionist's eyes widened as he reached in his back pocket, pulled out his checkbook, and wrote a check for the entire balance. "I would appreciate it if you could mail me a copy of everything here," he said.

"Yes, sir. Should I mail it to Kelli's address?"

He nodded.

She handed him a small card. "This is Ruth's next appointment."

Logan glanced at the card and placed it in his wallet. "Thank you."

He had turned to go when the woman stopped him. "Mr. Sinclair?"

"Yes?"

"These are Ruth's prescriptions. Kelli usually takes them."

Logan took the slips and managed a smile. "I'll take them. Thanks again." Then he rejoined his aunt and Kelli outside. "Well, ladies, since it's almost noon, how about I treat you both to lunch?"

Kelli noticed the prescriptions in his hands and grimaced. "I'm sorry, Logan, but I've got a million errands to run. Why don't you treat your aunt? She hasn't eaten out lately." Kelli started to step toward the walk, when she suddenly stopped and held out her hand. "Since I'm headed back into town, I'll get those filled for Ruth."

Logan casually placed them in his pants pocket. "That's okay. I have a couple things to pick up anyway. Ruth, could you show me where the pharmacy is?"

"Mercy yes, I've lived in these parts for the past forty years. I'm sure I could still find Sanderson's." Ruth turned to Kelli. "Are you sure you can't join us?"

Kelli knew defeat when it was staring her in the face. Logan was determined to get Ruth's medication. With any luck, he'd pay the bill without asking any questions. "Not today, Ruth. You and Logan have a real nice time and catch up on some gossip."

She was almost inside her car when Logan stopped her with a gentle hand on her shoulder. "Kelli, please join us."

Without turning around, she cursed her lack of luck. Two minutes more and she would have made her exit without Logan seeing the tears about to fall. She had failed. The more she tried to balance Henry's and Ruth's Social Security and meager pension checks with the accumulating medical expenses, the further behind she got.

She suspected Logan had just settled Dr. Young's account. But there was also an outstanding balance at Sanderson's Pharmacy. Not to mention the balance still owed to the dentist and optometrist. Both sets of dentures and Ruth's glasses had been lost in the fire, and their *charming* cousin Edwin hadn't seen the need to have them replaced. Kelli regretted not having enough money to help them more.

She quickly put on her sunglasses and shook her head. "I'm sorry, Logan, but not today. I have a million things to do before Fairyland opens next month. You and Ruth enjoy yourselves."

Logan frowned as he watched Kelli climb in her ancient Chevy and start the engine. "Thank you for letting me know about Ruth," he said. "It explains a lot."

Kelli couldn't trust her voice, so she nodded and dropped the gearshift into reverse. She had to get out of there, fast. Tears were slowly making their way down her cheek as she turned away from Logan.

"Tonight, after dinner, I would like to talk to you, if it's convenient?" Kelli's "Fine" was muffled as she pulled the door shut and backed up.

Logan stood in the middle of the street and watched as Kelli backed her car into a driveway three doors down, jammed it into drive, and took off in the opposite direction.

"Is something wrong, Logan?"

He smiled reassuringly at his aunt. "No, nothing's wrong. Kelli just had a lot to do." He slowed his steps to match his aunt's and lovingly placed her in the front seat of his rental car. As he rounded the front of his car, he looked in the direction Kelli had taken. Why had she purposely reversed halfway down the block when she could have driven straight forward? And why hadn't she looked at him?

Kelli dried her tears. She was a fool and she knew it. She had done it royally this time. She'd fallen in love with Logan. With a frustrated oath, Kelli punched the steering wheel, then she blew her nose in the last tissue. She had driven two miles out of town before her tears forced her to pull over. When had she fallen in love? Kelli wanted to know the exact moment it happened. She leaned her head back against the vinyl seat, closed her eyes, and thought. When a woman fell in love for the first time in her life, she expected certain things. There should be a sign: blazing fireworks, a two-hundred-piece orchestra playing Beethoven's Fifth Symphony. Something.

Right now, all she had was a sinking feeling in the pit of her stomach.

She took off her glasses and looked into the mirror. Mascara was streaked down her cheeks and her eyes were red and swollen. She could add looking like a demented raccoon to her "falling in love" signs.

Late, late, late. Kelli parked her car next to the school's pickup truck in Fairyland's parking lot and rushed out of the car. Mr. Weedle, the school's carpentry teacher, was a stickler for punctuality, and she was already late. She ran to the theater, out of breath by the time she arrived. A group of husky teens was busy ripping out rotted benches while Henry and Mr. Weedle were sitting on the stage pleasantly discussing which type of bait was best for catching trout.

Kelli was shocked. Here she had broken the speed limit to make this meeting, and Mr. Weedle was chatting with Henry as if they were long-lost buddies. She took a deep calming breath and walked over to them. "Hello, Mr. Weedle. I'm sorry I'm late."

"No problem, girl." He didn't notice Kelli's grimace at being called "girl." "Henry here has been filling me in on what has to be done. It's about time you got some *real* help around here."

Kelli ignored the sarcastic remark, just as she'd been doing for the past five years. She smiled pleasantly. "Henry's in charge of the grounds. He'll show you where there are some logs that would make nice benches."

"We've already seen them, girl."

Kelli closed her eyes and counted to ten. "Well then, if you need me, I'll be in my workshop."

She was about to walk away when Henry asked, "How did it go?"

A flush of pink crept up her cheeks. "I'm sorry, Henry, my mind was elsewhere. Everything went great. Logan took Ruth to lunch and the doctor said she is as fit as a fiddle."

"How did Logan take it?"

"Amazingly well. I'm afraid I chickened out and stayed in the waiting room while the doctor explained everything. He seemed calm when he came out and Ruth was smiling." Kelli smiled at the older gentleman. The man owned a piece of her heart. "I'll go fix some lunch, come in as soon as you have things straightened out here."

Henry frowned as he watched Kelli head slowly toward the parking lot. Something was wrong. He noticed how she bristled when George Weedle called her "girl," but there was something more. He knew she'd told him the truth about the appointment. Kelli would never lie, especially about Ruth's health. So why were her shoulders slightly slumped? And why was the spring missing from her step? He turned toward George. "If you can manage on your own, I think I'll go get lunch." Then he headed toward the house behind the young woman who had become so important to him.

"I'm telling you, son, if I didn't know better, I'd swear she was sulking."

Logan glared at his uncle. "Why are you two assuming I have anything to do with it?"

Ruth ran nervous fingers over her apron. "We

didn't say you did, Logan. It's just that Kelli's acting strange."

"How?"

"She doesn't sparkle."

Privately Logan agreed with his aunt's assessment, but he'd eat spinach before admitting it. "Maybe it's a full moon, or maybe the planets are misaligned. Lord, the woman believes in fairies— there is no telling what's upsetting her."

Henry pulled out a kitchen chair and sat down. "She was fine this morning when she left with Ruth. When she came back for the meeting with George, she was upset."

Ruth checked on the chicken roasting in the oven then sat down next to Henry. "She was fine at the doctor's." She thought for a moment longer. "Until she turned down your invitation to lunch."

"Are you trying to tell me I upset her by inviting her to lunch?"

"Of course not, son. It just seems funny that she turned you down and then hurried on home after saying she had errands to run."

Logan took a deep breath. "So what would you two like me to do about it? Avoid asking her to lunch?"

"No," said Ruth, "we want you to be especially nice to her. Dinner will be ready in a few minutes, so go out to her workshop and get her."

Logan stood up and scowled at his relatives. He muttered a few choice words under his breath as he walked out of the kitchen and headed for the workshop. This was not his day.

He'd nearly gone into shock earlier when the doctor explained about his aunt's heart. When he learned that she'd been under the doctor's supervision for the past eight years, he'd felt guilt pressing on his chest. Eight years! Where in the hell had he been during that time? In some god-forsaken country working on his tan.

He jammed his hands deeper into the pockets of his jeans and marched up to the warped door of Kelli's shop. He forced himself to relax. The person who'd shouldered his responsibilities, *his* responsibilities, had been Kelli. Sweet, beautiful, kissable Kelli. When he returned from lunch with Ruth, he had seen her in the shop painting the last of the statues. Henry was right, the sparkle was gone. Her eyes had held an "I lost my puppy" look.

Determined to be witty, cheery, and totally charming, Logan threw open the door. "Kelli, how would you like to see my shorts? They have cute little bunnies all over them."

Kelli made herself concentrate on the plate of food in front of her. She could feel Ruth's and Henry's curious glances, but every time she looked up she saw only Logan. He was sitting across from her innocently eating his dinner, as if the scene in her shop had never happened. At his grand entrance, Kelli had spun around and dropped her paintbrush. He had swaggered into the room with his chest puffed out and white teeth flashing. She had taken one look at his strut and burst out laughing. All the way back to the house she begged for a peek while he pretended to be offended by her mirth.

"Aunt Ruth, you really outdid yourself tonight," Logan said. "The chicken is delicious." A spark of mischief gleamed in his eyes as he looked at Kelli. "Kelli, would you please pass the carrots, I have this uncontrollable craving for some."

Kelli bit her lower lip to prevent a giggle from escaping. She picked up the small relish tray, and passed it.

Logan wiggled his nose in thanks.

She choked on a laugh. Ruth and Henry were still giving her strange looks. First they had been as careful around her as if they were walking on eggshells, now they looked ready to commit her to the funny farm.

Logan was the only one enjoying himself.

Well, Kelli decided, two can play this game. She slipped her sneaker off under the table and rubbed her foot on Logan's calf. "Some more peas, Ruth?" Kelli asked innocently.

Logan felt her toes massage his leg, reaching higher and higher. He gulped, and dropped the forkful of stuffing that was halfway to his mouth.

Ruth looked at him, concerned. "Logan, are you all right? You look a little pale."

Logan glared at Kelli, but her head was bent down, as she continued to eat her dinner. He moved his leg away from her. "I'm fine, Ruth."

Kelli looked up, her eyes sparkling. "I don't know, Logan. You do look a little furry around the edges."

Henry and Ruth exchanged curious glances as a tide of red swept up Logan's cheek. With a shrug of their shoulders they finished their meal and retreated into the living room, leaving the kitchen to the odd couple.

Logan waited until the door swung shut. "You shouldn't play with fire."

There was an innocent gleam in her eyes as she purred, "I thought it was bunnies I was playing with."

He pulled her chair out. "If your foot had gone any higher, it would have met Thumper."

A silent O formed on her lips. He pulled her up against him. "You still don't understand what you do to me, do you?"

Kelli gazed into his desire-filled eyes and melted. She could feel the heat of him. His body was pressed against her and his strong arms held her. He might not love her, but he wanted her. Was it enough? Somehow she'd make it enough. Her arms encircled his neck, and she whispered his name. "Logan."

He was lost. He lowered his head and captured the lips that had spoken his name so softly. Heat pounded through his body as he plunged his tongue deep into her mouth. Lord, how he wanted this woman.

Kelli purred with satisfaction and pressed in closer. She felt his hands pull her hips against his hardening body and groaned when he broke the kiss. "Feel what you do to me. All you have to do is look at me and I get aroused." He placed a kiss on the tip of her nose and watched as she opened her passion-darkened eyes. "Kelli, what am I going to do with you?" He smiled ruefully. "Don't answer that. I know what I would like to do, but it's not going to happen." He gently lowered her arms and backed up a step. "Ruth and Henry are on the other side of that door. If they knew what I was thinking, they'd throw me out of here. They love you like a granddaughter."

"The feeling is mutual."

Logan tenderly ran his thumb over her moist, swollen lower lip and sighed. "They think you could walk on water if you wanted to. Don't you see, you're their savior. You were here when they needed someone. I wasn't. You're open, kind, and generous to a fault."

"Logan?"

He heard the bewilderment in her voice and quickly dropped his hand. "Don't be generous with me, Kelli." He backed up to the coat rack and grabbed his coat. "I don't deserve it."

She watched as he opened the door and stepped outside. "Logan, you're wrong," she called. She felt filled with sadness as the door closed behind him. She wasn't sure what had happened. Did he think she was being generous by melting into his arms? Was her generosity wrong?

Five minutes later Ruth found Kelli scouring the dishes and generally slopping water all over the place. Kelli looked furious.

"Where's Logan."

She had heard Logan's car pull out of the drive moments after he walked out. "He wanted to take a ride."

"Didn't you want to go?"

"No, I'm almost finished with the painting. A couple more hours tonight and I'll be done."

Ruth picked up a dish towel and started to dry the dishes. "That's wonderful. Now you will have time to relax."

Kelli muttered an appropriate response as she glared out the kitchen window. Sure, she'd relax. Just as soon as she murdered a certain someone who thought she was too generous with her body.

Kelli jerked up in bed and became instantly awake. A quick glance at the clock showed it was after two in the morning. What woke her? As another sound reached her ears, fear clutched at her heart. When Logan still hadn't returned by twelve, she had gone to bed. The doors were unlocked as always; but even Logan couldn't be making that much noise downstairs.

She slipped from her bed, nudged Tinkerbell awake, and reached into the closet for a weapon. The only thing she could find was a lacy pink parasol. She stepped out onto the landing and glanced into the darkened living room. Nothing.

Four steps later she was standing by Logan's empty bed when she heard the sound of a chair falling over in the kitchen, followed by a bellow of pain. Good Lord, what was going on down there?

Kelli raised the parasol, shoved Tinkerbell in front of her, and quietly made her way downstairs. When she was halfway across the living room, she heard Josh laugh. She hurried the rest of the way, threw open the kitchen door, and stopped dead in her tracks.

Josh was leaning nonchalantly against the counter making instant coffee while Logan sat in the middle of the kitchen floor rubbing the back of his head.

"What is going on here?" she demanded.

Logan blinked at the three Kellis swirling in front of him and wisely kept his mouth shut. Josh reached for another cup and poured a coffee for Kelli. He placed Logan's on the floor next to him and handed Kelli hers. "Guess who I brought home?"

Kelli gaped at Logan. "He's drunk!"

"Sloshed to the gills."

"Tell me he didn't wreck his car." Logan seemed to be in one piece, except that he kept rubbing the back of his head.

"You think I would let him drive?"

"You were with him?"

Josh walked over to the table and sat down. "Since eight o'clock."

Kelli grimaced as she watched Logan take a sip of his coffee. "Then why aren't you drunk?"

"Haven't you ever heard of a designated driver?"

"Yes, but Logan doesn't seem like the type to plan to get wasted in some bar." With dawning horror she looked at Josh. "Tell me you didn't take him to Bronco Bill's." The look on his face told all. She groaned. "How could you, Josh? For Pete's sake, he is Henry's nephew."

"Dammit, Kelli. It started out harmless enough. I figured I'd spike a few of his drinks to loosen him up."

"Why?"

"I wanted to know what kind of man he was. After all, you were taking a bath with him the other day!"

"Maybe you should be checking out my morals instead?" she muttered. She glanced in sympathy toward Logan. "It looks like he had more than a few spiked drinks."

Logan finished his coffee and studied the two spinning Kellis. His vision was improving, but his hearing had a way to go. What were Josh and Kelli arguing about? What in the hell had been in those drinks?

"Well, once he started talking, it got real interesting."

Kelli slammed her half-full mug on the table. "What got interesting?"

"Sorry, love, it isn't my place to tell you." Josh grinned.

"Tell me what?"

Josh rose to his feet and placed his and Kelli's cups in the sink. "There are certain times in a man's life when he's entitled to get drunk."

Kelli rose to her feet and shouted, "Such as?"

"His bachelor party."

"Logan's not getting married."

"Loss of a loved one."

"No one died, Josh, *yet*."

Josh heard the hostility in her voice, but he didn't think she was as upset as she sounded. "How about shore leave?"

"Logan's a geologist, not a sailor."

Logan wanted to agree with Kelli, to tell them he wasn't a sailor, but didn't want to call attention to himself. As long as she ranted and raved at Josh, he was safe. Logan didn't want the full force of that temper turned on him. Somewhere in the back of his mind he knew Josh was the cause of him sitting on the kitchen floor. Revenge—namely having Kelli yell at the officer—was sweet.

"Listen, Kelli," Josh said, "I can't tell you any more. It isn't my business."

"You just can't leave him sitting there."

"Come on, I'll help you put him to bed. How he's still conscious is beyond me. I've never seen anyone drink ten Bronco Bill specials and still stand."

She placed Logan's arm across her shoulder and with Josh's help managed to pull him to his feet. "He had ten of those death traps?" She looked at him in sympathy.

They successfully navigated the hazardous trip up the stairs. "He actually had eleven," Josh admitted.

Kelli issued a string of curses on Josh's head, his future children's, and into the seventh generation, as they maneuvered Logan into his room. With Josh's help she managed to get Logan out of his clothes, except for a pair of white boxer shorts that boasted comical pink rabbits.

"I don't know, Kelli. The man has strange taste in underwear."

Logan smiled as Kelli tenderly pulled up the

comforter beneath his chin and tucked him securely into bed. He opened his eyes and focused on one wavy Kelli. "You got to peek after all."

She placed a kiss on his forehead. "Yes, Logan." She looked directly at Josh and sweetly said, "And tomorrow you get to kill Josh."

Logan muttered, "Good," as sleep overtook him.

Seven

Logan made the final adjustment on the carbu- retor of Kelli's lawn tractor. He smiled in satisfac- tion. The ancient, rusty pile of bolts was purring like a kitten once again. Two days earlier Logan had thought Snippy had seen its last days. But Kelli had looked so crushed and anxious that Logan had promised to do what he could. Twenty hours and a small fortune later, Snippy was roar- ing to go.

With great care Logan closed the once shiny green hood and wiped his greasy hands on a rag. Test-run time. Time to put the smile back on Kelli's face.

For the past four days they had been circling each other, acting friendly and polite but not really talking. When he had opened his eyes Tues- day morning, Logan saw Josh standing next to his bed with a tall drink in his hand.

"Which direction to the elephant graveyard?" Logan asked, gripping his throbbing head.

Josh hid his smile and handed Logan the

drink. "Drink this and I'll promise within half an hour you will be back to normal."

"I'm not sure but I think you're responsible for the chain saw in my head."

"Afraid so."

Logan pulled himself up to sit on the edge of the bed. "Then why in the hell would I drink anything you hand me?"

"Because if you don't, my best friend will never speak to me again."

"Kelli?"

"Yeah, the little tyrant who is in the kitchen this very minute still ranting about doing unspeakable things to some of my favorite body parts."

A visible shudder shook Josh's frame. Logan would have smiled, if his lips didn't hurt so badly. He eyed the drink with a great deal of speculation. He couldn't possibly feel worse. Logan raised the glass and downed it. "You realize that I owe you one?"

Josh smiled with understanding as he took the empty glass. "Paybacks, huh?"

Logan closed his eyes as his stomach rumbled against the concoction he had just swallowed. "When you're least expecting it, I'll be there. From the way I'm feeling, it won't be a pretty sight."

Josh headed for the door with a full-blown grin plastered on his face. "I don't have to worry. Kelli would never allow you to do something totally degrading to me."

"What does Kelli have to do with it?"

Josh winked knowingly. "Her opinion matters too much to you."

Logan raised an eyebrow.

"You're in love with her," Josh explained.

Logan had watched Josh stroll from his room

and groaned. What had he said to make Josh think that?

As Logan climbed on the mower now, he was positive he'd never told Josh he was in love with Kelli. He still hadn't figured out what his feelings for Kelli were. He respected and applauded her courage. He understood her desire for a family and sympathized with her feeling to be needed. The work she did for the drama club was admirable, and the time and energy she put into Fairyland was amazing. She had the body of a goddess, a face as fresh as the morning sun, and the most kissable lips he'd ever tasted. Every night, she plagued his dreams, stirred his body, and made his life hell. *But was that love?*

Logan maneuvered the small tractor over the rough dirt path and headed toward where Kelli was raking.

Kelli heard the sounds of the approaching tractor and smiled. Logan had fixed Snippy and hadn't even made a derogatory remark about its name. She dropped her rake on the ground and stretched. And thought.

Since the morning Josh had brought him home three sheets to the wind, Logan had been acting very helpful, friendly, and polite. She had expected the worst when Josh showed up to check on Logan; instead they became friends. Within an hour of Josh's arrival, Logan was showered, dressed, and eating a hearty breakfast. Afterward he and Josh put on boots and unjammed the massive log from the creek. The friendliness continued after Josh left for work, with Logan insisting he was having fun clearing unwanted logs and branches.

That had set the pattern for the days that followed. Logan managed to show up every morning in the kitchen moments after her, always wishing her a pleasant morning and inquiring if there was anything special he could do to help around Fairyland. They both worked outside from sunup to dusk, only stopping briefly to grab a quick lunch. Dinner was a four-way conversation centered around Fairyland: What was done, what must be done, and what should be done. After the dishes were washed and Ruth and Henry headed toward their cottage, she and Logan cleaned the house. It was mutually agreed that Ruth wasn't to know who was cleaning, and if she believed it was the fairies, no harm was done.

Saying good night to Logan was the hardest part of her day. Every evening he sat at her kitchen table with a preoccupied expression, perusing a stack of magazines and doing two-finger typing on her old portable typewriter. There hadn't been any more stolen kisses or mention of bunny skivvies.

In short, life had been the pits.

Kelli sighed and picked up her rake as Logan came around the bend and waved. She saluted back and quickly stepped out of his way as he brought the tractor to a halt. His smile was contagious. "You did it. You fixed Snippy," she said.

"Of course. Did you doubt it?"

"Not for a moment." She lovingly placed her hand on the hood. "When can I try her out?"

Logan couldn't resist the excitement twinkling in her gray eyes. His arms ached from not holding her and his body cried out for her warmth. His smile held the wistfulness of a man and the power of the devil as he slid back, and gently patted the seat in front of him. "Hop on up and we'll take her for a spin."

Kelli arched one fine golden brow, trying to look

undecided. But the rhythm of her heart increased as she thought about being nestled so close against Logan. Was this his way of making an overture, or was he just being friendly? *Come on, she told herself, this is your big chance. Climb on up there, and if all he wants to do is shift gears, you could accidentally drive him into the creek.* "Isn't it going to be a little crowded?"

Logan smiled wickedly. "I'll try to control myself."

Kelli took a step closer and muttered under her breath, "That's what I'm afraid of."

"Did you say something?"

"No." Kelli was almost ready to grab his helpful hand when Tinkerbell came charging out of the woods. She watched with amusement as the dog made a beeline straight for the tractor, barking furiously. "Stop that, Tinkerbell."

Then the dog jammed her nose under the tractor and started to dig.

"What is she after?" Logan asked.

"I didn't see anything. Maybe it was a chipmunk?" Tinkerbell let out a howl and continued to tunnel under the idling mower. Kelli tried to pull her dog away and was rewarded with a growl. In exasperation she blew the whistle. Kelli blew three times before Tinkerbell paid attention. "What is with you, girl? There's nothing under there." Kelli suppressed her laugh as Tinkerbell sat proudly in the middle of the path with her tongue hanging out panting.

With a loving pat Kelli praised Tinkerbell. "Good girl."

In the darkness beneath the tractor a cotter pin dropped unnoticed to lie in the dusty soil. A four-inch spring followed and rolled into the small hole the dog had dug. The air was still as a piece of brass linkage swung wildly for a moment before slowly coming to rest against the dented crankcase.

Kelli jumped back as Tinkerbell shot to her feet wildly barking. In a flash, Tinkerbell crashed through the surrounding woods in pursuit of the unknown.

Logan laughed as Tinkerbell disappeared from sight. "Did you see what she was after?"

"Afraid not. Whatever it was I'm sure it got away."

He reached out and gently captured her hand. "Come on, my lady, your chariot awaits."

Kelli ducked her head to hide the pleasure she felt when he called her "my lady." She settled in between his thighs and felt his arms tighten around her waist. "Are you sure this is going to work?" she joked.

Logan felt his body's immediate reaction to her closeness and silently groaned. "Trust me. You're going to do all the driving, I'm going to sit right here and hang on. Place your feet on the brake and clutch and it's all yours."

She expertly took the controls and started down the path. Snippy bounced with vigor as it plowed over dips and valleys. The rocking motion set off friction where their jeans were connected. With every jerk of the tractor his hands bounced from her stomach to beneath her breasts, and back down. She was amazed at how she could feel every movement of his fingers through a flannel shirt and a zipped-up sweatshirt. A fiery blush tinted her cheeks as her breasts grew heavy and her nipples hardened.

She tried to concentrate on maneuvering Snippy around any gullies or sudden dips. "She runs like a champ, Logan," she finally said. "Thank you."

With a sudden intake of breath, Logan groaned as Kelli's sweet bottom connected with a part of his anatomy that never knew how exciting mowing the lawn could be. His voice was husky as he whispered in her ear, "You're welcome."

Kelli felt his breath caress her neck and shuddered. With a sudden twist to the wheel she headed the tractor toward the pond, the closest route home.

Logan felt her shiver and tightened his hold. He resisted the temptation to kiss her delicate neck. "Cold?" he asked.

The wheel slipped from her trembling hands as Logan's lips nipped at the sensitive skin of her exposed neck. Recovering herself, she wildly grabbed the wheel and slammed on the brakes as the tractor bolted down a grassy hill straight for the pond. *Nothing!* The mower was picking up speed at an alarming rate. "Logan!" she cried fearfully.

From behind her he reached quickly, smashing her foot with his, trying to hit the brakes. Nothing! What in the hell had happened? Seeing the cold water of the pond come rushing closer, he yelled, "Jump!"

Kelli caught a blurred look at Logan's determined face before he stood up and jumped, pulling her along with him. Soft, moist soil cushioned her fall as she landed a few feet from the water's edge. Laying flat on her back she turned her head and watched, astonished, as Snippy splashed into the pond. Then the engine died. The heavy tractor started to slowly sink into the mud.

"Kelli, are you okay?" Logan asked, staring at the sight.

"Yes." Kelli looked at the five inches of her tractor still above water and silently laughed. She turned her head and stared up at Logan, who was leaning over her. "I don't think Snippy knows how to swim."

"Lord, I'm sorry, Kelli." He tenderly wiped a streak of mud off her cheek. "What happened? The brakes were working perfectly before. Are you okay? You didn't break anything when you jumped, did you?" He cautiously ran his hands up both of her jean-clad legs and started on her arms. "Don't worry about Snippy, I'll fix her again."

"Logan?"

"Yes?"

Kelli's heart almost burst with joy. Logan did care! He was blabbering about broken bones and a water-logged tractor. With a loving smile she said, "Shut up and kiss me."

He gazed down at the woman whose hips he was straddling and grinned. His lips were a mere inch away. "I thought you'd never ask," he murmured. With warm tenderness he gently took her mouth.

Desire, already kindled, blazed into a raging inferno. She ran her tongue over his lips. Heat curled within her as he opened his mouth. A satisfied purr escaped her throat as he deepened the kiss and shifted his weight across her. She felt the hard evidence of his arousal pressed against her thigh and gloried in the knowledge he found her desirable.

Logan groaned as Kelli arched her back and pressed her breasts against his chest. With a sudden movement he rolled onto his back, bringing her with him. Kelli ended up straddling his hips, tormenting him out of his mind. With sure fingers he slowly lowered the zipper of her gray sweatshirt.

The look of concentration on Logan's face held her spellbound as he lingered over every button on her flannel shirt.

As her buttons were eased open, the need to have Logan touch her grew. Cool air caressed her heated skin as he slowly parted her blouse to reveal the white satin camisole she wore underneath. Desire burned in his gaze as he watched her darkened nipples harden. Twin peaks broke the smoothness of the shimmering satin. With the lightest of touches, he touched her.

Kelli sucked air into her lungs, and released it, crying his name. "Logan."

His pleasure turned to distress as he noticed the small mud streak that covered her breasts. He raised his mud-smeared hand and groaned. He was covered with mud, so was Kelli. They were lying in the dirt about to make love. With awe he glanced up and met Kelli's darkened eyes. He *was* in love with Kelli SantaFe! When had that happened? More important, *what* was he going to do about it? He watched as the desire in Kelli's gaze turned to confusion. With a sigh, he tenderly pulled her down and lovingly cradled her in his arms. He and Kelli would not make love for the first time in a field of mud. There would be satin sheets, roses, champagne, and endless hours.

Kelli listened as Logan's rapid heartbeat slowed. What had happened? One moment flames had ignited wherever he touched and moisture had gathered between her thighs. The next instant she was hauled into his arms while he whispered soothing words. His hands created a warm friction as they massaged her back, and his chest was the best pillow she'd ever rested her head on. Didn't he feel the same jolt of recognition whenever they touched?

Humiliation washed over her as Logan noticed her whimper of distress. "Shhh, babe, it's okay." A groan escaped him as he felt the woman in his arms stiffen. Gently placing a hand under her chin, he forced her to look at him. "It should be quite obvious that I still want you. In case it hasn't occurred to you, we happen to be lying in mud. Personally I have nothing against mud, but what we feel for each other deserves better than a quick roll in the grime." Seeing the uncertainty on her face, he asked, "Don't you agree?"

A huge grin spread across her face. He hadn't actually said he loved her, but he did just admit to some kind of feeling. Feelings so powerful that fondling each other in the dirt upset him. In surprise she realized that Logan was a romantic. He probably was looking for candlelight, dreamy music, and French perfume, while she'd supplied mud facials. How could she tell the man she loved that none of those things mattered? Material possessions never impressed her, it was the things that held no monetary value that captured her heart. With love shining in her eyes she leaned closer and whispered, "Yes," against his lips.

Kelli and Logan returned home late in the afternoon covered with mud and smiles. Ruth had raised an eyebrow at their explanation, but didn't comment. Logan graciously allowed Kelli to use the shower first as he sat down to enjoy a cup of coffee with his aunt.

Ruth checked on the roast slowly browning in the oven. She grabbed a bowl of potatoes and two peelers before sitting down across from Logan. She handed her nephew a peeler. "I'm really happy to see you and Kelli getting along."

From the tone of her voice, Logan knew it was lecture time. He started to skin a potato and waited for his aunt to continue.

"Did Kelli ever tell you about the day we met?"

"No, she said it wasn't her story to tell."

"Humph! It's more her story than ours." Ruth glanced down her nose and studied the potato she held. "You already know that Edwin came here to get us out of Suzette's hair. She was having some kind of bridge party. Anyway, while we were here I started to have this attack. Henry got me to a bench and with the help of a nitro pill everything was under control."

"Nitro! You never told me about the nitro pills."

"Of course I did, Logan. Even the doctor told you I was taking medication. What kind of medication did you think I was taking?" Ruth looked at Logan's bewildered expression and chuckled. She started to pull a silver chain from around her neck. "See what Kelli gave me for Christmas." Instead of a charm, a tiny vial was linked through the chain. "It's a nitro holder. This way I'll always have my medicine with me and I won't have to dig through my purse to find it."

Visions of his beloved aunt clutching her chest while searching through a crammed handbag for her life-saving medicine sent shivers down his spine. "Not only is Kelli beautiful, she's smart."

"Yes, she is. As I was resting on the bench Edwin started to rant and rave about being inconvenienced. Henry told him I needed the rest but Edwin wouldn't listen. There was a terrible scene. Edwin was shouting, Henry was begging, and all I could do was cry. That's how Kelli found us.

"The sight of Kelli emerging from the woods like some avenging angel had me reaching for the nitro bottle again. She was dressed in one of her fairy outfits with wings and silver glitter in her hair. I thought I had died and gone to heaven."

"What happened?"

"She took in the scene with a glance. Henry explained to her that our house had burned down and we were staying with Edwin until we located you. She said she had a spare bedroom and we were welcome to stay with her. End of story."

"Just like that?"

Ruth chuckled. "Logan, at my age I've become a pretty good judge of character. Who would you pick to live with, Kelli or Edwin?"

Logan started to peel another potato. "Okay, so we both are experts in judging character. Now you can tell me whatever is on your mind."

"Obvious, was I?" Seriously, she said, "You do know that we love you like a son?"

Logan's hand stopped in mid-peel. "I hate it when you start conversations with that line."

"Henry and I have also grown to love Kelli like a daughter. We don't want to see her get hurt."

"By me?"

"I might be half-blind, but I can see the way you two look at each other. You will hurt her when you go back to Afghanistan."

"What if I don't go back to *Sudan*?"

Ruth laid down a half-finished potato and stared at Logan's sincere expression. "You remind me of your father when you look at me like that. Frank always wore that expression whenever he was about to make a sacrifice for the good of the family."

"Dad? What did he sacrifice?"

"His dream. When he was a little boy, he wanted to be a pilot. By the time he was old enough to decide on his future, World War II had broken out. Uncle Sam didn't care about a young man's dream; Frank looked like infantry material. After the war when our father died, Frank became the main support of the family, working in the steel mill. Then he met and married your mother, and within a year you were born."

"And he never flew."

"No. He was in an airplane a few times, but I don't think it was the same. When I had the heart attack we didn't tell you because I was afraid you'd come home and give up *your* dream. Henry and I kept my health problems from you because we love you."

Logan saw the tears in his aunt's eyes and reached for her hand. "Thank you, but it wasn't necessary. Being a geologist is my dream, not working in Sudan. I can be a geologist in the States."

"You said you work with oil."

"Yes, but I can work in other areas."

"In case you haven't noticed, this isn't Texas where there are oil wells every hundred feet."

"I noticed." He gently squeezed her trembling hand. "I said I could be a geologist in the States, not necessarily Pennsylvania. It could mean a move."

"Would this *move* involve Henry and me?"

"I can't force you to come with me. I would *like* you to come." Noticing her frown, he said, "Nothing is settled yet. I'm still in the résumé stage, seeing what's available out there and where. All I ask is that you think about it."

Ruth nodded her gray head. "What about Kelli?"

As if on cue, Kelli swung open the kitchen door and entered the room in time to hear the last question. "What about me?"

Logan couldn't meet her eyes. "Ruth was just asking if you hurt yourself when you jumped from the tractor."

Her heart sank. He didn't want her to know what he was doing. The man she loved had lied to her. With a grimace she glanced down at her finest red silk blouse and newest jeans. Her hair was freshly washed and streaming down her back. Delicate gold studs dotted her ears, the barest traces of makeup darkened her eyes, and a light flower scent followed her. Who was she trying to impress? Surely not the man sitting in front of her with the guilty look on his face. "No, Ruth, I didn't get hurt. Shower's free, Logan."

He knew he was caught in the small lie, but this wasn't the time or the place to go into his career plans. Tonight after Ruth and Henry retired, he'd have a talk with Kelli. *If I can keep my hands off her for that long. She did look gorgeous with that touch of fire in her eyes.* With a small shake of his head, he rose and walked toward the door. "Thanks, Kelli, I hope you saved me some hot water."

Kelli tapped her foot as she glared at Logan. He was busily making up a tray with coffee and oatmeal cookies. She followed him into the living room and purposely sat in the chair farthest away from him.

He hid his smile. "Thank you for graciously listening to me." By the time his aunt and uncle left the kitchen, Kelli had built up a head of steam that was ready to explode. "Would you like a cup of coffee?"

"Yes, please." She might need something to throw at him, she reasoned. Kelli noticed that he fixed the coffee exactly as she liked it, but didn't comment on it.

He cautiously handed her the cup and sat back down on the sofa. "I lied to you earlier." She raised an eyebrow. "When you walked into the kitchen Ruth and I weren't talking about you jumping off the tractor."

"No? What were you talking about?"

"Dreams."

"Whose?"

"My father's mostly." In a nervous gesture, Logan picked up and then quickly replaced his cup. "Can I start at the beginning and get back to the dreams?"

Intrigued by his nervousness she took a sip of her coffee and nodded her head.

"I want to start by thanking you for everything you've done for my aunt and uncle. Aunt Ruth finally told me what happened the day they came to Fairyland. I'm ashamed to admit that Edwin is a blood relation, twice removed."

"You're not responsible for your relatives, any more than I am for mine."

Surprised, he asked, "You have a family?"

"Yes, Ruth and Henry are my family. My relatives abandoned me at the hospital when I was a baby."

Logan could have kicked himself for bringing up families. "I'm sorry." A sadness dulled her eyes as she reached for a cookie. "I know you've been helping them pay their bills."

"The agreement was, when their insurance money came in from the fire, they'd reimburse me."

"Is there fire insurance?"

Kelli drank the remainder of her coffee. "I'm a worse liar than you are. No, there's no insurance.

They finally contacted me this week. Ruth hadn't kept up with the premiums. Their policy was canceled over a year ago."

"That means you won't be reimbursed."

"I didn't do it to be reimbursed. They're my family now, and I take care of my family."

"No, Kelli, they're still my family. You love them, and they love you, but they are my responsibility."

Sadly, she shook her head.

"I paid the balance due Dr. Young, Sanderson's Pharmacy, and their dentist. Was there anyplace else they owed?"

Pride kept Kelli's lips sealed. There was no way she would tell him about the optometrist.

Logan knew she was holding something back and sighed. "Look, Kelli, I'm not going to force any revelations from you. And I won't force them to move. I'm not sure about my future, so there's nothing to offer them, right now. Later, they will have the chance to make up their own minds. They're two caring, loving individuals, whom I love very much."

Hurt swept through her as she stood up and faced Logan. "If you love them so much, where were you when they needed you?"

Logan allowed the pain to wash over him. She was right. He had ignored his responsibilities. He had come home like some crusading hero and had expected everything to fall into place the way *he* wanted it to. Now, his family was being torn apart and he had fallen in love with the person he was hurting the most.

Kelli regretted the accusation as soon as she made it. "I'm sorry, Logan, I have no right to judge."

"Yes you do. You're right, I didn't handle things well. I should have known something was wrong when I didn't receive any mail from them. I figured they were becoming forgetful, and I'd be coming home soon anyway. I didn't live up to my responsibilities." He reached for a folder lying half under the tray of coffee. "I spent some time figuring what it has been costing you to keep them here." Logan opened the folder and pulled out a check. "Please accept this with my sincere thanks."

Kelli looked down at the check Logan had placed in her hand. He was trying to pay her off! He was putting a price on the love she shared with his aunt and uncle.

He watched as the color drained from her face and realized he had just made the biggest mistake in his life. "Kelli?"

Slowly and carefully Kelli tore the check in half, then in half again. She let the pieces flow through her fingers, to the floor. "You are to have your bags packed and be out of my house by tomorrow morning." Then she slowly made her way upstairs to the sanctuary of her room.

Eight

Kelli pulled the pillow over her head and groaned. What in the world was all this ruckus about? It sounded like someone was playing demolition derby in the living room. She half opened one eye, nudged the pillow, and glanced at the illuminating red digits on her clock. It was three o'clock in the morning and her house was being trashed. Great, what else could possibly go wrong with her life?

With a colorful oath she tiptoed to the closed door. An exasperated sigh escaped her lips as she stepped over Tinkerbell, who growled in her sleep and shifted into a more comfortable position. Obviously, she wasn't going to join her. *So much for the calvary*, she thought. As silently as possible she opened the door and slipped out onto the landing.

Amusement lightened her expression as she sat on the top step and watched the bizarre scene below. Logan, dressed in a pair of jeans, was trying to coax Moth down from the top shelf of a bookcase. "Come on, boy, be a good kitty and come down." With an arrogant tilt of his head, Moth pushed a thick volume containing the history of American art off the shelf.

Kelli silently admired Logan's fancy footwork as he caught it in midair. He turned to place the heavy book on the couch when Moth deep-sixed the Renaissance period. "Dammit," he whispered furiously. "Cut that out, you stupid cat. You're going to wake Kelli, and then there will be hell to pay." Logan bent over to pick up the fallen book as Moth sent a small book on Leonardo da Vinci toppling over the edge.

Kelli clamped a hand over her mouth as she watched the book harmlessly bounce off Logan's bare back. What had gotten into Moth?

Logan held the book in his hands carefully watching for Moth's next move. The sound of shattering glass had Logan dashing over to the coffee table trying to save what was left of the tray of coffee they had used earlier. He gingerly stepped over the shattered mug and lifted the tray out of Mustardseed's way. "What in the hell is with you guys tonight? Did you get into catnip or something? If Kelli comes down, she'll think *I* did all this. I'm in enough trouble with her, without your help."

Mustardseed sat on the arm of the sofa attentively listening to Logan's every word. "Please tell your buddies here to knock it off," Logan said to the cat. "I don't relish the job of telling Kelli her cats are schizo, she's mad enough as it is." He watched Mustardseed cock his head as if patiently waiting for him to continue. "All I wanted to do was make things easier for her. She works so hard for so little. Did you know that Mr. Wheedle said the whole town was betting against her and Fairyland when she first started it?"

Logan shook his head. Why was he talking to a bunch of cats? Moth laid on the shelf, watching his every move, Mustardseed was listening attentively, and Cobweb had jumped down from the top of the china closet.

As long as he kept talking, the cats seemed calmer. He wondered if this is how the Pied Piper felt. With a cautious step closer to the front door he lowered his voice. "The drama club swears she's part fairy and Dan Teeterman is half in love with her." Logan watched as Moth jumped from the shelf and sat on a chair closer to him. "Josh says that Kelli could stretch a nickel further than anyone he ever knew. He also says she's proud and stubborn and won't accept help from anyone."

Logan took another step toward the door and smiled as Mustardseed moved closer. "The way I figure it, guys, is, if Fairyland is running in the black, Kelli SantaFe is part fairy." He stepped closer to the door and held the knob in his free hand. "Ruth and Henry love her like a daughter. I can't blame them, she inspires that in people." He opened the door and chuckled as all three cats sashayed forward. "I didn't mean to insult her with the check. I wanted to be fair. I wanted her to know that I will take financial responsibility for my aunt and uncle."

One giant step had Logan standing outside while the three cats were sitting on the doorsill. With an imploring gesture for understanding Logan said, "I'm not what's known as a good catch. I don't have a job, I come complete with an elderly aunt and uncle, Lord, I don't even have a place to live." He took another step backward. "When you get serious about a woman, you want to show some endearing characteristics." With a self-mocking chuckle, he said, "I guess I blew that one."

Kelli gripped the doorknob harder and swallowed the lump that had formed in her throat. She had followed Logan's progress across the living room listening to every word. By the time she reached the bottom step he was out the door encouraging the cats to follow. Two tears ran down her cheeks as she stepped from behind the door. "No, you didn't blow it," she said.

"Kelli!"

"Shouldn't you be saying all this stuff to me, not to a bunch of schizo cats?"

Logan glanced down sheepishly. "Don't you guys have mice to catch?" He watched in surprise as the cats raised their tails and strutted off into the nearby woods. His gaze turned serious as he walked toward Kelli. "There's a lot I should be saying to you, but every time I open my mouth, I seem to choke on my foot."

Kelli backed up into the room and allowed Logan to shut the door behind him. She swiped at her eyes and mustered a small smile. He was the sweetest man alive. The whole time he had been pouring his heart out to a bunch of furry felines she had come to understand him better. Love was all-consuming, all-forgiving. "If you start to choke, I'll give you mouth-to-mouth."

He placed the tray down on the coffee table and glanced around the room. Books and broken pottery were scattered across the floor, throw pillows were dragged from the couch, and Ruth's weeping fig plant was tilted at a peculiar angle. Curtains were pulled from their tiebacks and a table lamp was lying on its side. With a frown he righted the lamp. "I didn't do this."

"I know."

He bent to pick up a pillow. "How long were you listening?"

Her breath caught in her throat as she eyed the play of muscles across his tanned back. When he straightened, her gaze was drawn to the fine dusting of hair that covered his chest. Saints preserve her, but what that man did for skin ought to be illegal. "I came in about the time Moth was trying to beat some art into your head."

Logan looked at her lovingly, finally noticing her outfit. "This is the first time I've ever seen you when you weren't wearing red."

Kelli glanced down at the huge fluorescent green T-shirt with "A Midsummer Night's Dream beats Freddy's Nightmare" written across it in bold black letters. The nightshirt came to mid-thigh and covered everything vital, but a blush still stained her cheeks. "The drama club sells the shirts during the presentation of the plays to help raise money for costumes and scenery."

Logan's mouth went dry as his gaze dropped from her shirt to glide down long silky legs. His voice was husky. "You look good in green."

"Thank you." When the silence stretched she asked, "Did you mean what you were saying to the cats?"

"Yes. I was going to explain again in the morning when you cooled down a little." He took a hesitant step closer. "The check wasn't intended as you thought."

A womanly smile curved her mouth. "So I found out. Are you going to rewrite it?"

He thanked his guardian angel for this second chance. He vowed not to mess it up again. "No, we'll leave the past where it belongs. However, as long as I'm living here, I would like to pay for any of our expenses."

"I can live with that."

"Thanks, but can you live with the fact you have three deranged cats?"

She chuckled. "I guess I'll have to, they've lived here longer than me. I don't know what got into them tonight, they've never done anything like that before."

Desire burned in his eyes. "Can you live in the same house with a man who wants you constantly? I wake up in the morning aching for you. I spend my days planning ways to bump into you." He ran a trembling hand through his hair. "I spend my nights praying for the strength to keep from opening your door and joining you in bed."

Kelli stared at him. "Why?"

He took a step closer, lifted his finger, and tenderly brushed at a spot of moisture left by her tears. "I've never felt like this before. I'm afraid once I make love to you, I won't be able to leave your bed."

A wondrous smile curved her lips as Logan softly cupped her cheek. A warm tingling sensation radiated from his touch as he slowly threaded his hand into her hair. "Would that be so bad?" she asked weakly.

"I can't offer you any promises."

Kelli heard the honesty in his voice and understood. Here was a man who would give her the truth. How could he offer promises when his own life was at a crossroad? She could be safe and walk away from him now, or she could risk it all . . .

She took the biggest step of her life, straight into Logan's arms. With a seductive glance she whispered, "I don't remember asking for any."

Logan groaned and pulled her further into his embrace. Heat coiled low in his body as Kelli's soft mouth pressed a kiss against his collarbone. "You won't regret it." A light caress of her lips on his shoulder brought a moan to his lips. "I'll protect you. You do know that I'll never intentionally hurt you, don't you?"

For a long moment Kelli pressed her cheek against his chest. Raising her face she smiled lovingly. "Logan?"

He was lost. He took one look at the expression on her face and felt the love for this woman engulf him. He tenderly brushed back a tendril of golden hair and sighed. "Ummm?"

"Shut up and make love to me."

Logan chuckled and swept her up in his arms. "Your wish is my command." He switched off the lamp and headed for the stairs.

He felt Kelli snuggled deep against his chest as he climbed the steps. He hesitated outside her door. "Does this mean you don't want me to talk while I make love to you?"

She tightened her hold on his neck and forced his mouth closer. "While we make love, you may say anything you please." A wicked pout curved her mouth. "But I did have plans for those lips."

Logan captured her pout in a heated kiss as he opened her door and carried her over the threshold . . .

Three cats sat in a flower box with their noses pressed against the living room windowpane. As the door closed behind the couple, they turned to each other as if to say, "Not bad for a night's work." With what appeared to be a sense of camaraderie they jumped down and headed for the woods.

*   *   *

Kelli blinked when Logan found the light switch. She slowly slipped from his arms and backed up a step. She was nervous. Her feelings were stronger than they had ever been before, exciting, and utterly irresistible.

He read the apprehension in her eyes and reassured her with a smile. One step brought him within touching distance. He gently rubbed his finger across her lips. "We'll take it slow and easy." Moist lips opened and her breath fanned his finger. Her small pink tongue darted out between even white teeth and teased his heated skin.

Kelli watched his expression as she ran her tongue down the length of his finger. With the confidence of a woman in love she gently threaded her fingers through the fine dusting of hair covering his chest. The rapid beat of his heart spurred her on as she ran her hands down the silky mass and encountered the denim barrier.

With a growl Logan picked her up, stepped over Tinkerbell, and fell onto the bed. His mouth was demanding as he plunged his tongue deeply into her mouth. Her sweet gentle tongue answered his and he turned the commanding kiss into a tender merging. Hunger surged through him as she pressed closer and ran heated hands up his back.

A warm moisture settled between her legs as the length of his hardness rhythmically pressed against her outer thigh. With the instinct born to Eve she opened her thighs and nestled him through the barricade of clothes.

He groaned and pulled the nightshirt over her head without breaking their lower body contact. A scrap of black silk and a metal zipper was all that was separating them. He had promised her slow and easy and protection. A ragged sigh escaped him as he slowly stood up.

Kelli blinked in confusion for a moment. Her bewilderment cleared as he slowly lowered his zipper and peeled his jeans and shorts away. *This was a man in his full magnificence who proudly stood in front of her and waited her response.* Appreciation and love gleamed in her eyes as she pushed down the covers and patted the sheet next to her.

He released the breath he'd been holding and lay down. His voice was husky. "You're beautiful," he whispered. With tenderness he took her mouth in a kiss that promised more than words ever could.

Kelli wrapped her arms around his neck and answered every one of those promises.

The kiss deepened as Logan gently ran his hand up her stomach to cup her breast. A flick of his thumb brought the hardened peak to sharp attention. He felt the sweet moan Kelli uttered as he broke the kiss.

Heat scorched her skin from Logan's gaze as he worshiped her breasts with his eyes. "They're perfect." With a gentle caress he held one globe in the palm of his hand. "See, they were made for me."

Kelli looked down at his tanned hand. "Yes, perfect," she agreed. Fascination held her still as Logan bent his head and pulled the nipple deep into his mouth.

He heard her cry of passion as he bathed the nub with his tongue. Her petite fingers dug into his hair and her hips gently jerked. Turning his head he gave the other breast the same tantalizing treatment. He ran a quivering hand over the satiny smoothness of her hip snagging the delicate black panties.

Kelli didn't feel him relieve her of the last barrier. Warm, skilled fingers drew small circles up her thigh and drew closer to the aching heat. When they were on the verge of reaching their goal, Logan stopped and started to torment the other thigh. Her voice carried a mixture of frustration and desire as she sighed, "Logan."

He released the moist nub from his lips and raised his head. A sexy grin lit up his face. With maddening calmness he asked, "Yes?"

Kelli read a wealth of knowledge in that grin and decided the game worked both ways. Her hand lightly fluttered over his lean hip to rest on his hard thigh. Her small delicate fingers softly brushed the fine curling hair dusting his thighs. She heard his breath catch as her fingers teased the dark thatch that surrounded his maleness.

A hoarse plea reached her ears. "Kelli?"

With tender strength she wrapped her fingers around his silken arousal. She felt the grip on her wrist as he dislodged himself from her hold.

His breath was ragged. Logan kissed the palm of her hand and placed it on his shoulder. A seductive smile broke across his mouth as he bent to kiss away her pout.

Flames erupted as he deepened the kiss and softly caressed the golden curls that guarded her womanhood. A moan escaped her as his tongue entered her mouth the same instant his seeking finger found the moist center of her being. He released her mouth and kissed the twin peaks brushing his chest.

The sucking motion of his lips matched the sweet thrusting of his finger. Need built within her as she raised her hips to meet his thrusts. "Logan, please!"

In one fluid movement he rolled over and retrieved a foil packet from his jeans. He quickly prepared himself and knelt between her thighs. She gave him a smile of appreciation. With deliberate slowness he entered the moist haven. When he was completely sheathed he closed his eyes and waited for Kelli to adjust.

She felt the satin length of him inside and sighed. Completeness washed over her as she wrapped her thighs around his hips and felt him move. Her hands clung to his shoulders as she met his every stroke. As the rhythm increased she strained against him and murmured his name. "Logan."

He kissed his name from her lips and replaced it with hers. "Kelli, open your eyes."

She tossed her head from side to side and fought for breath. It was there in front of her, she could feel it, almost touch it. With certainty she knew Logan could take her there. She opened her eyes and looked up into his blazing eyes. "Logan, I . . ." There it was. "I . . ." She could touch it. "I . . ." She held it. "I love you." In that moment of blind bliss she locked eyes with him and knew he felt it too.

Logan held the sleeping woman in his arms and gently brushed her hair back. A tender smile touched his mouth as he lovingly kissed her forehead. *Oh, Kelli, what have we done? There wasn't supposed to be any promises.* How could he make any decision about his life with Kelli in his arms? *Simple, you idiot,* he told himself, *they will include her.* What if she doesn't want to be included? *She loves you, doesn't she?* Yes, but that doesn't mean she'll be willing to follow in his footsteps.

There was no sense beating his head against a wall, until he knew what he was facing. The only one who could tell him that was sleeping in his arms.

Interest sparked in his eyes as he stared around her room. Could the unorthodox place hold the secret to her heart? When he had entered the room hours ago, he knew it was different. He just hadn't paid attention to it. Now lying in her bed he stared in wonder at the scenes greeting him. On the front half of the room where the ceiling slanted, she had painted two huge skylights. One was a night scene with twinkling stars, while the other portrayed a bright rising sun.

The room was furnished with only a double bed done completely in white, desk, nightstand, and a bureau. A pale green carpet was on the floor and white ruffled curtains hung at the only window. Amusement gleamed in his eyes as he studied the door to her closet. She had painted a door opening into another room with another door opening into another room. Logan counted five doors painted within her one, and smiled. Unusual, yet showing a great deal of talent. He was turning his head to another scene when something struck him. All five painted doors, and the real one had different doorknobs. *He wondered if it meant anything?* He'd have to ask.

Then he grinned at the whimsical mural across the full wall. Kelli had drawn a closet, this time with the door open. Red dresses hung haphazardly from the bending bar inside. Hats, boxes, and an array of female clutter crammed the shelf above the bar. Shoes, socks, boots, and umbrellas littered the floor. On the back of the door crookedly hung was a black evening dress.

A white rattan chair was painted next to a potted palm. There was even an open book as though someone had thoughtlessly left it behind. The rest of the mural depicted bookshelves. From floor to ceiling they were crammed with books, knick-knacks, and other paraphernalia.

Logan smiled as he reached over and turned off the lamp. Kelli was extremely talented. The quality of her work was amazing, so real, but so fanciful. The details were so lifelike that he'd swear every one of the books painted on those shelves had titles. He gently cradled Kelli deeper into his embrace and wondered why she would paint a closet, when she already had a real one. Something about that question bothered him as he drifted into sleep.

Kelli awoke when a gentle kiss landed on her navel. She slowly opened her eyes and stared at the light brown mop of hair nudging her stomach. Her nipples were hardening as Logan ran his hand up the back of her knees. She wondered how she could be so comfortable with Logan? Last night after their first explosive joining she had held him tight and savored the afterglow. When she had felt a movement deep inside she had raised questioning eyes. His sexy grin had been answer enough as they tenderly and slowly made love again.

Her voice held the huskiness of sleep and desire as she asked, "Enjoying yourself?"

Logan chuckled against the satiny smoothness of her stomach. "No. I was hoping you were an early riser."

She glanced at her clock. "It's *four-thirty*."

"Really." He placed a swift kiss on the end of her pouting nipples. "Do you want to go back to sleep?"

She laughed and pulled the white sheets over their heads. "No, but I want to know why you didn't wake me earlier?"

A sigh of ecstasy left her lips as Logan's reply was mumbled against her thigh.

Forty minutes later she felt Logan slip from beneath the wrinkled sheets. "Where are you going?"

"Someone has to clean the living room before Ruth gets here."

Kelli yawned, and said, "I'll help you."

Logan looked at the delectable picture Kelli made and smiled. Her golden hair was tousled and spread out across the pillow. Her lips were swollen and reddened from his kisses and a flush tinted her cheeks. An eyelet-trimmed white sheet was discreetly pulled up over her breasts, but left one of her creamy thighs bare.

With a disgusted chuckle he felt desire rekindle. He knew this was going to happen, he even told her. How could he possibly leave this woman when she wore the expression of having just been thoroughly loved?

He saw the fatigue in her large gray eyes and quickly leaned over and placed a light kiss on the end of her nose. "No. You stay here and catch some sleep. I'll clean up the mess."

"Sure?"

He pulled on his jeans. "Positive."

Kelly heard the door close behind him and mumbled something as she drifted to sleep.

Logan stood at the side of her bed and gazed down at the inviting picture she made. Her creamy arms held the pillow he had used and one dusky nipple peeked out over the sheet. Soft dew-kissed lips were slightly parted in sleep and dark lashes lay against her cheeks. Lord, she was beautiful.

Forcing down the desire burning in his stomach, he gently shook her shoulder. "Kelli." The only response was a disgruntled mutter, so he shook her harder. "Kelli."

"Hmmm . . . ."

"We have a problem."

She nestled deeper into the pillow and asked, "What?"

Logan gingerly sat down on the bed next to her. "Are you awake?"

Kelli groaned into the pillow. She felt the soft object being taken away and forced her eyes open. "Now I am."

"Good. I just went downstairs to straighten up, and guess what?"

"Lord, Logan,"—there was exasperation in her voice—"don't play guessing games with me at five o'clock in the morning."

"The room wasn't messed up."

Kelli blinked. "Huh?"

In a voice reserved for parents lecturing naughty children, he said, "The room is spotless. No broken cup, no books scattered around." He ran a hand through his disheveled hair and raised his voice. "Even the plant is perfect."

"So?"

"So!" He leaped from the bed and gawked at the woman lying there. "How can you say 'so.' Someone has to have cleaned up that mess."

She yanked up the quilt to bury her head. "Ruth or Henry must have come in and cleaned it."

"Kelli, it's five-thirty in the morning. They aren't even up yet."

"Neither was I, until you came in here ranting about nothing."

Incredulous, he roared, "Nothing?"

She lowered the edge of the quilt and glared at the towering hunk next to her bed. "Listen, you are putting a damper on the morning after. I didn't clean the room. You didn't clean the room. That means either Ruth or Henry cleaned it."

Logan knew she made sense, but couldn't help asking, "Are you sure?"

With total exasperation she raised her arms. "No, Logan, thousands of pixie-faced fairies came in and cleaned it." She watched as his mouth fell open, and she shook her head. "They also pay the mortgage, repair the car, and spin straw into gold." With a frustrated groan she pulled the covers back over her head and wiggled deeper into the mattress.

The bed shifted as Logan stood up and turned out the light. A cool breeze caressed her leg as Logan placed a moist kiss on her ankle. "Logan?"

"Hmmm."

When his lips tickled the back of her knee she asked, "What are you doing?"

"Making your morning after something to remember." Kelli purred as his lips glided up her thigh and gave her something she'd remember for the rest of her life.

Nine

Kelli bit into her tuna-fish sandwich and scowled at the empty chair across from her. "Ruth, where you did you say Logan was?"

"All he said was to tell you he'd be back by lunch."

A glance at the clock proved he was wrong. It was two minutes after twelve and she missed him. She had awakened reaching for him, only to come up empty-handed. While she had showered the gentle ache of sore muscles brought a smile to her face. *The man was thorough, there wasn't one inch of her body that had escaped his attention. And what gorgeous attention it was!* She had hurriedly dressed and headed downstairs to find that Logan had left an hour earlier. Where she didn't know. Where could he have gone at eight in the morning?

The sound of an approaching truck brought Kelli out of her daze. She placed her uneaten sandwich back on her plate, grabbed a handful of chips, and headed out the back door with Ruth and Henry on her heels.

Logan climbed out of his car and gestured to the truck driver. Kelli watched with astonishment as a huge stake-body truck, from the local lawn-care dealership, parked and two men got out. Without breaking their stride they lowered a ramp and drove a brand-new lawn tractor off the truck bed. A heavy-duty utility cart and a double-bag grass catcher followed.

"What is that?" Her voice cracked.

"It's a tractor," Logan said.

With eyes wide with horror she shrieked, "Whose?"

This was going to be as tough as he thought. He ran an exasperated hand over the back of his neck and smiled pleasantly at the two delivery-men. He grabbed hold of her arm. "Excuse us for a moment," he told the men as he dragged Kelli back into the house.

The instant the door closed she found herself pressed against Logan's body. His lips captured the sound of the protest she was about to utter.

Melting heat curled in her abdomen as his tongue slipped into her mouth and mated with hers. Her arms encircled his neck while her breasts flattened against his chest. Moisture gathered at the junction of her thighs and a purr sounded at the back of her throat.

A light nip to her swollen lower lip ended the kiss and Logan whispered, "Good morning."

Dissatisfied at the abrupt ending she muttered, "It's afternoon."

A glance at his watch caused a smile to break across his face. "So it is." He softly caressed her flushed cheek. "I missed you. It's been five hours since I held you."

"Five hours and twenty-two minutes." She could

have told him the seconds, but why get technical. "I missed you too."

His mouth was closing in for another kiss when she asked, "Whose tractor is it?"

Logan sighed. "Yours." Before she could voice any objections, he said, "Don't go jumping to conclusions. What happened last night has absolutely nothing to do with the tractor. If I thought for one minute you'd be pigheaded enough to believe that, I would drive the stupid thing into the pond and let it sink."

Kelli said the most intelligent thing she could think of. "Oh!"

"Face it, Kelli, Snippy isn't as young as she used to be. She's not equipped to handle the kind of work that has to be done to keep Fairyland running." Seeing the hurt expression darken her eyes, he said, "You don't have to haul her to the dump, just be more selective in her chores. I bought everything I need to get her running again."

"I can't afford—"

"I know." Logan pulled two slips of paper from his shirt pocket and showed them to her. "Here's the receipt for the tractor. It's paid in full and in your name." Feeling her distress, he continued, "It seems like a lot at first glance, but consider it's the top of the line and warranted for three years. Plus they threw in the grass catcher and cart free."

"I still can't afford it, Logan."

"Yes you can." He showed her the other piece of paper that had scribbles across it. "See, I figured it out. You could pay me back a small amount every month during the tourist season. In a few years the tractor will be paid for."

Kelli glanced at the final monthly payment and

raised an eyebrow. "That's it?" He nodded. "*How* many years?"

"Five," he mumbled.

She sighed. Five years of payments. A brand-new tractor with a cart. No more using the wheelbarrow for transporting wood. It was so tempting. "What about interest?"

Logan hid his smile. He knew she'd be hell to convince. "Since the money was sitting in an ordinary savings account, I only charged you five and a half percent." There was no way he'd allow her to make payments for the next five years, but first he had to get her to accept the tractor. He'd figure out a way to stop the payments later.

She sank her teeth into her lower lip and studied the paper clutched in her hand. It was a godsend, but since she hadn't received many of those in her life she hesitated. The payments seemed ridiculously small, but even small payments have a way of looking monstrous when the checkbook reads zero. She reread the amounts and knew she'd never get a better deal. She already planned on going out to work immediately after Fairyland closed for the season. With Ruth and Henry, expenses had skyrocketed and the meager income Fairyland provided couldn't support all three of them. Kelli calculated that if she worked for those five months every year, they would manage just fine. A smile curved her mouth; she could even meet the payments on her new tractor.

"I'd do it, on a couple of conditions. Number one, don't you ever again buy anything else for me or Fairyland without my approval."

"Agreed to the Fairyland stipulation, but I'll buy you whatever I want. I just won't buy you anything pertaining to business."

Kelli smiled at her first victory. "I also want the

payment schedule drawn up legally, so I can sign it."

Logan smiled as he ran his thumb over her lower lip. "Agreed to, Counselor. Are you sure you never wanted to be a lawyer?" Her "Positive" was muffled against his lips. When the kiss threatened to engulf them, he slowly concluded it with a series of light nips. "That was to seal the bargain."

"I thought that had nothing to do with us?"

He leaned forward and kissed the corner of her mouth. "It doesn't, but you have irresistible lips." With a subtle movement of his lower body he said, "You have quite a few things that are irresistible. If we didn't have a crowd of people standing outside this door, I'd show you what every one of them was."

A teasing light gleamed in her eyes as she opened the door and whispered, "Promises, promises."

Kelli and Logan spent a busy afternoon hauling debris. The new tractor, which Kelli lovingly christened Patton after Ben's hero, ran like a champ. After dinner they played a game of checkers for the benefit of Ruth and Henry, who enjoyed their lighthearted banter. When the elderly couple retired for the evening, Kelli and Logan made quick work of any chores that needed to be done. He had shooed her into the bathroom with a kiss.

When the shower started Logan made a quick trip to the car and then headed for Kelli's room. The water was still running when he entered the bathroom and joined her.

Kelli felt the draft of cold air as the shower curtain moved to allow him to step into the tub. Her arms were raised, working conditioner into her hair. Without opening her eyes she said, "Logan?"

His voice held a husky chuckle. "Whom else were you expecting?"

"I wasn't expecting anyone," she murmured as she stepped under the spray.

His heart pounded and the breath caught in his throat as the water cascaded over her body. *She looks like a water nymph. I wonder if they're members of the fairy family?* Her breasts were high and firm as she ran her fingers through her hair. A slim waist and a womanly flare of hips tapered off into luscious thighs, shapely calves, and dainty toes complete with red toenail polish. His gaze was drawn to the mass of wet golden curls at the junction of her thighs. Desire flared in his abdomen and his body stirred into arousal. He picked up a bar of soap and lathered her back.

After her initial surprise she relaxed into his massaging hands. Warmth spread through her limbs as the exotic combination of soap, water, and Logan filled her senses. When Logan had first stepped into the tub she had felt self-conscious and nervous. *I'm standing under bright lights, completely naked, with a stringy mass of soaking wet hair. That's it, girl, entice the socks right off him. Be alluring, sexy, and soggy. It drives men into rages of passion.* A small smile tilted up the corner of her mouth as she looked over her shoulder at the man who was spending an extremely long time on one little back.

The heat of his gaze caused the level of steam to rise as she took the bar of soap from his hand. With gentle small circles she worked a lather into his chest, over his shoulders, and down bulging biceps.

He closed his eyes as delicate fingers worked their way up hardened thighs. When the tips of her fingers gently stroked his rigid manhood, he groaned and pulled her into his arms. "Enough!" He hauled her under the water with him and sputtered, "Lord, woman, you're dangerous." As the last of the suds sailed down the drain he turned off the water and stepped out of the tub with her in his arms.

He carefully stood her on her feet and wrapped her in a fluffy green bath towel. Reaching for the other towel he started to tenderly dry her hair. "Where's your hair dryer?"

"Under the sink." As he retrieved the dryer, she got another towel from the closet and patted his back dry. The blast of hot air whipped her hair around as she continued to blot him dry.

Logan bit his lip and silently groaned as Kelli patted an extremely sensitive area. "Enjoying yourself?"

Kelli dried the responsive spot for the fifth time and murmured, "A woman's work is never done."

Dry golden hair cascaded down her back as he picked her up, turned off the light, and carried her into the bedroom. She was snuggling his neck when the perfumed scent of roses enveloped her. Raising her head she stared in awe at the dozen long-stemmed red roses sitting in a crystal vase on her dresser. "Oh, my!"

Logan grinned at the look of joy on her face. "Yep, all yours."

She was about to thank him properly when a flash of silver caught her attention. Next to the bed sat an ice bucket with a bottle of champagne sticking out of a mound of ice. Two delicate-looking glasses sat near the bucket. With a raised eyebrow she asked, "Are you trying to seduce me?"

In a devilish voice he said, "Yes, is it working?"

She threw her arms around his neck and kissed him. Slowly breaking the heated kiss, she whispered, "Yes."

Logan felt the only barrier between them slip down her breasts. With one quick tug he dispensed with the towel and placed an adoring kiss on each of the pouting nipples. He walked the two paces to the bed and lowered her to the turned-down sheets.

Kelli let loose a shriek when the icy coldness of the sheets connected with the heated skin of her back. "Dammit, Logan."

He studied the woman, who had flown back into his arms, as she pointed down at the bed. What the hell? Nothing was there except brand-new shimmering white satin sheets that still held the crease marks from the packaging. "What's wrong?"

"What are they?"

A frown pulled at his brows as he asked, "You don't like satin sheets?"

Kelli hid her smile against his chest. "I wouldn't know. I've never slept on any."

"Then what's the problem?"

"Where did you have them, in the freezer?"

"No, the car." With dawning horror he reached down and felt the sheet. "Yep, they're still nippy around the edges. Sorry about that."

He is a romantic. Roses, champagne, and satin sheets, what could be next? With an indignant sniff, she said, "Sure you are, it wasn't your bottom hitting the iceberg."

Logan let out an Indiana war cry and flopped down on the bed, still cradling her in his arms.

Kelli heard his sudden intake of breath and giggled. She squirmed about until she was positioned perfectly on top of him. Placing her elbows on his chest, she raised her head and smiled down at him. "Gee, Logan, these sheets are great."

Gritting his teeth, he muttered, "Be quiet, and stop moving around."

She grinned and wiggled her hips at a persistent bulge that was nudging the inside of her thigh. "I think I feel the tip of the iceberg?"

Logan groaned and pulled her mouth down for a heated kiss. As the kiss intensified, he quickly prepared himself and settled her seeking hips over him.

Kelli slowly lowered herself and sighed. "Nine tenths was below the surface."

Logan replaced the empty bottle in the bucket of melted ice and hugged the woman at his side closer. "I told you the sheets would warm up."

She couldn't decide if she preferred the rich sinfulness of the cool sheets or the rough, warm strength of Logan. A secret smile curved her lips as she snuggled closer to him. No contest. "Warm up? I was wondering if they were flame retardant."

A chuckle vibrated deep in his chest as he shifted his weight and pulled her deeper under the quilt. "Flames, hmmm . . . you say the sweetest things."

"It's the champagne talking."

He nipped at her lower lip and murmured, "You're sure you never had champagne before?"

"Positive. I would have remembered the bubbles." She sighed as his lips trailed down her neck. "I've also never received red roses. Thank you, Logan."

He forced his mind off the luscious body beneath

him and concentrated on the woman. *She'd never had roses, champagne, or satin sheets. Lord, where are the men around here? Didn't anyone ever notice the woman beneath the fairy costumes?*

With a gentle brush of his finger, he pushed a stray piece of hair off her flushed cheek. He gazed down into her smiling gray eyes and said, "I love you, Kelli SantaFe."

She blinked and stared up into the sincerity shining from his darkened eyes. He did love her. Joy radiated from her as she wrapped her arms around his neck and with a tear-filled voice whispered, "I love you."

Logan kissed away the drop of moisture from the corner of her eye. "Please, Kelli, don't cry. I know we have a lot to work out, but *we will work it out.*"

"I wasn't crying about that. I always cry when I'm happy."

He placed a tender kiss on the end of her nose. "Then I better buy stock in the company that makes Kleenex, because I plan on making it my life's mission to see you're always happy." He captured her sigh of contentment and turned it into a moan of ecstasy.

Logan glanced up from his mail and smiled as Kelli walked into the kitchen. She was dressed in a sparkling white leotard with a silvery-threaded sheer billowing skirt. Her hair was braided into a coronet with silver ribbons running through it, and a pair of shimmering wings completed the outfit. "You look sexy as hell."

She glanced down at her fairy outfit and curtsied. "Thanks, but I wasn't trying for sexy. I have a group of sixty-three first-graders arriving in one hour."

"I still can't believe you have seven tours lined up already and you're not officially open."

"That's okay, I'm not officially charging them." With a shrug of her shoulder she asked, "Is everything set up by the theater?"

"For the third times, yes." He chuckled and said, "You're not used to delegating. The tables for the drinks and cookies are up."

She leaned down and kissed the corner of his mouth. "Thanks."

"How do you expect to make a profit if you don't charge for the school tours? The small amount you do charge only covers the cost of the punch and cookies you provide."

"I couldn't live with myself, if I had to make a living off six-year-old kids." A dreamy smile lit her face as she said, "Wait until you see their faces. It's magic. For one day they're allowed to believe in fairies, pots of gold, and magical kingdoms underground."

Logan stared at her expression and saw the magic. He tenderly traced her cheek and said, "You believe, that's why they believe."

Kelli felt a fiery blush sweep up her cheek and quickly turned toward the refrigerator. She opened the door and said, "Grown-ups don't believe in such rubbish."

He studied her back as she poured herself a glass of milk. *Maybe grown-ups don't believe, but Kelli did.* During the past two weeks they had become friends and lovers. They had worked side by side during the day getting Fairyland ready for its opening the next Friday night, when the drama club would present *A Midsummer Night's Dream.* Each evening she had helped type his correspondence to an array of different companies, and had listened to his hopes and fears for his career. The nights were spent in each other's arms.

With a glance at the letter still in his hand, he asked, "What do you think of Utah?"

"Utah?" A thoughtful expression crossed her face as she answered, "Salt, Mormons, and a bunch of large white-toothed singers come to mind. Why?"

"I just received a request for an interview there next week."

Kelli fought the panic threatening to overpower her—Utah was over two thousand miles away. *He's asking your opinion, be supportive and understanding. Oh, hell, tell him not to go.* "Is it what you've been looking for?"

He glanced from her confused expression back to the letter. "It's more. I won't be part of a team, I'll be heading it."

She plastered a smile on her face. "Congratulations, I say go for it."

Logan placed the letter on the table, stood up, and walked over to her. He gently cupped her chin and raised her face for his inspection. Tears were sparkling in her eyes as he asked, "What's wrong? Don't you like Utah?"

Kelli bit her lip and rapidly blinked her eyes to keep the tears from falling. With a ragged sigh, she said, "I'm going to miss you."

Logan laughed as he hauled her into his arms. "It will only be for a couple of days. I'll be back before you'd miss me."

With the warmth of his arms supporting her she voiced her deepest fear. "Not then. I'll miss you when you move there."

He stiffened and backed up a step. Looking into her eyes he said, "You'd be coming with me."

Startled, she asked, "Me? Why?"

"Because it's customary for a husband and wife to live together."

Kelli opened her mouth; when nothing came out she snapped it shut.

Marriage! He was talking about marriage, families, and happily ever after.

He was talking about giving up Fairyland and moving to Utah. She gazed up and locked eyes with the man she loved. She'd move to Afghanistan to be with him—how much worse could Utah be? Still mad at the panic he'd caused in her, she said, "You could at least have asked me."

With a flourish, Logan knelt on one knee and gently grasped her cold hands. "Kelli SantaFe, will you do me the honor of becoming my wife?"

Her face radiated love as she said, "It would be my pleasure." The next instant she found herself being kissed senseless, wrapped in his secure arms. A giggle escaped her as Logan muttered an oath concerning the wings attached to her back.

A series of small nips ended the kiss and he stepped back and promised, "We'll finish this later. Your guests will be arriving in twenty minutes and I told Ruth I'd help her pass out the cookies she baked." His hand was gentle as he secured a wayward curl into her braid. "Lord, I can't believe I just proposed to a fairy."

Kelli beamed and lovingly kissed his cheek. "It's my glamour." She walked to the door and said, "I have to go, I'll see you at the cookie table later."

He started to pick up the mail, then stopped. "Kelli, do you want any children?"

"Hundreds," was followed by a kiss blown from her fingertips as she shut the door.

Logan swallowed the lump that had formed in his throat. *She did say hundreds, didn't she? Impossible, no woman could have hundreds, but then again Kelli wasn't your average woman. Two kids would be nice. A boy to carry on the name and a darling girl who believed in fairies and was the spitting image of her mother.* He placed the mail on top of the refrigerator and headed out the door. *Then again, four kids had a nice ring to it.*

Kelli greeted two busloads of loud boisterous children with a smile. This was the best part of owning Fairyland, guiding a youngster into his imagination. Teachers and homeroom mothers gladly turned the tour over to her as she quickly assembled sixty-two antsy six-year-olds on the benches in the theater.

Logan sat spellbound at the rear of the theater as Kelli told stories about some well-known fairies. She was magical. The children listened wide-eyed to every word she said. She told them tales of Irish chieftains and the fairy hills of the Tuatha De Danann and a mischief-maker named Robin Goodfellow. She explained how a fairy was invisible to a person, unless it wanted to be seen, and why never to step into a fairy ring.

He watched as she captivated every child with legends of heroic deeds and the power of love. The children cheered the fairy knight, Midhir, as he won the mortal woman, Etain, from her evil husband. Loud hisses and boos were yelled at the Leshiye, the forest fairies of Russia, who were known for their nasty tricks. They listened as she explained how the world's population increase had caused some serious problems for the fairies of the world. There is no place they can call home. Since they are invisible to people, they live in constant fear of being stepped upon.

Kelli lowered her voice and said, "Five years ago a delegation from the F.F.F.F. came to my cottage and asked if they could take up residence on the property. Imagine my surprise when I could hold the whole entire delegation of twenty-five in the palm of my hand." She held up her hand and a collective sigh filled the theater.

"Ms. SantaFe, what does F.F.F.F. stand for?"

Kelli smiled at a teacher who had brought her first-grade class here every year since Fairyland opened. "It stands for the Freedom Fighters Federation of Fairies. Fairies are very patriotic and loyal to their country, they even have been known to go to war. Gremlins are members of the fairy family who made a name for themselves during World War I and II. These fairies love to tinker with machinery, especially aircraft. Since they are invisible they could cross enemy lines and do mischief to the enemy's planes. Unfortunately, the enemy had gremlins of their own, and many a good fairy lost his life during those wars."

Kelli looked out over the transfixed faces and smiled. "You got me sidetracked. Where was I?"

A freckled-face redhead shouted, "You were telling us how the fairies came here."

"Oh, yes. The delegation heard I lived alone and had plenty of room for their families. I immediately said they could, provided I could invite people to walk through and see if they could spot a fairy or two. They took a long time to talk this over between themselves before they agreed.

"We'll be starting our tour in a moment, so I want to explain the rules. First, and very important, don't leave the path. You could accidentally step on a fairy or squash their homes. Second, no running. Fairies are very tiny, and so are their legs. You could have the misfortune of running one down."

Logan chuckled as ninety percent of the children looked down and nervously shuffled their feet. Kelli raised her voice and said, "Line up with a partner. Two by two." As the teachers and mothers helped gather the children, Kelli waved to Ruth and Logan. With a beaming smile she asked the group if they were ready. As the roar died down, she started to walk into the woods to scout up fairies.

Logan and Ruth watched as the last child and teacher disappeared from sight. "She's wonderful with them, isn't she?"

A frown pulled at his mouth as he answered his aunt. "Yes, she is." Is this where his Kelli belonged, with the fairies and the children who came to see them? Was he wrong about Utah?

Kelli turned and answered a question a small girl had asked and chuckled at her grin, that was missing a tooth. First-graders were at the perfect age for Fairyland, still young enough to believe in the magic of the tooth fairy and Santa Claus. Every year the number of tours she performed increased as word spread from school district to school district. What would happen next year when she wasn't here? Who would spark the imagination of a child?

As she led the kids to a meadow where a fairy ring was visible she studied her surroundings. This was the only home she'd ever known and she loved it. She knew every tree, every inch of ground, and every animal. Who was going to take care of them when she was gone? What would happen to Angus, Caer, and their cygnets who were about to hatch?

With forced happiness she gathered the children near the ring and explained, "It's believed the ring is formed by dancing fairies. It is said if a person steps into the ring they will be imprisoned in the fairy world."

She chuckled as sixty-two pairs of eyes widened. "This one is totally harmless." With a light step she crossed over the boundaries of the ring and stood in the center. "See, there's nothing to fear from this one. Would anyone like to step in with me?" Sixty-two heads shook and one hundred and twenty-four little legs stepped backward. "Okay, maybe later." Out of the hundreds of students touring Fairyland each year, she'd only had two kids volunteer to step into the ring with her.

Kelli pointed out and named different trees and bushes along the way. She gave a brief talk on how baby trees start and grow and drew the kids' attention to a few bird's nests. She sighed as they reached the end of the tour without any fairy sightings, except for the statues she had positioned throughout the park. Last year two kids had earnestly sworn they had spotted a real fairy. The first child's teacher had written it off to the boy's imagination. When a second boy spotted a fairy two weeks later, his teacher assured Kelli he was the most honest and realistic child in her class. Kelli had smiled politely and said she understood those things, but on the inside she was fascinated. The boys came from different schools and even different towns, they didn't know each other, yet both boys' descriptions were identical.

Ten

"Logan, did you know that seventy percent of Utah's population is Mormon?"

He glanced up from an article in a journal he was reading. "So you informed me yesterday." With a gentle smile he reached for her hand. "Nervous?"

"Not unless Mormons still practice polygamy."

He folded his journal and placed it on the coffee table. With a light tug he pulled her into his arms. "Okay, short stuff, let's see the book." She snuggled against him and placed the encyclopedia on his lap. He pulled her closer as he glanced at the pictures of Bryce Canyon and Zion National Park. "Ever been camping?"

Images of a scared sixteen-year-old girl crossing the country on foot filtered through her mind. She had made it from New Mexico to Pennsylvania hitchhiking; she'd only accepted rides from families on vacations. She had been young, but not stupid. Many nights she'd slept out under bridges and on park benches. It really couldn't have been called camping. "No."

"Look at these mountains and canyons, they're

perfect for camping." His voice held a catch of excitement. "Have you ever seen country like this?"

"Yes, I was born and raised in northern New Mexico."

"Damn." He closed the book and dropped it on the table. He tenderly raised her chin and kissed her. "I'm sorry, Kelli. I didn't mean to bring that up. I thought you were raised in Pennsylvania."

"No. I didn't come east until I was sixteen."

"Why did you pick Pennsylvania?"

"I didn't. I was planning on Maine."

"Maine?"

She chuckled. "I opened a map and Maine was the state that was the farthest away. I was going to celebrate my independence with a lobster dinner and then get a job with a small fishing fleet."

"I take it you like lobster."

"Never had it."

He laughed. "Lord, woman, what am I going to do with you?" The answer was expressed by her suddenly darkened eyes. "Did I tell you I love you today?"

She felt the heat of his glance and melted. "Only twice."

Logan lowered her to the sofa and stretched out beside her. He traced her lower lip as lightly as a butterfly. "Tomorrow I'll call and cancel the interview."

"Why?"

"Because it upsets you. Utah is too close to memories you want to forget."

She was genuinely touched. He was willing to give up Utah because he thought it might upset her. Well, it did upset her, but not for the reasons he thought. How could she admit to a rational man like Logan that she was distressed for far different reasons. She'd read everything she could get her hands on about Utah . . . and not once were fairies mentioned.

"Don't worry," Logan said. "I got a very encouraging letter from Texas today. How do you feel about rodeos and snakeskin boots?" he asked in a serious tone.

A small giggle escaped her parted lips. *No doubt about it, he is the sweetest man alive, and he's mine.* "Logan, I want you to go to Utah and knock their socks off. I've dealt with my past, it's behind me now. This is the opportunity you've been waiting for. Go for it."

"Are you sure?"

"Positive. I'll even read up on camping while you're gone." She smiled devilishly. "Come to think of it, the sporting-goods store sells sleeping bags that zip together to form one large one. I always thought that sounded sinfully erotic."

"The hell with Utah, is that store still open?" asked Logan.

"It's ten o'clock at night."

He positioned a leg over hers and pressed her deeper into the couch. With unsteady fingers he slowly started to unbutton her blouse. "Please come with me to Utah for the interview."

Pleasure surged through her with every brush of his fingers. "We've been over this before. I can't. The play opens Friday night and I have to be here."

He moaned as he unfastened her lacy bra with a flick of his fingers. Her satiny smooth breasts were begging for his attention. He lowered his head, capturing a dusky peak with his lips and pulled it deep into his mouth.

Kelli arched her back and entwined her fingers deeper into Logan's thick hair. Excitement raced through her. She should be used to his touch, his kiss by now—but she wasn't. Every kiss was better than the first, his every touch excited her, and every time they made love she grew to love him more.

Raising his head, he looked down on her flushed face and said, "Three nights away from you. Lord, I'm going to miss you."

She rotated her hips, moving herself closer to him. "You don't leave for another two days."

In one fluid motion Logan stood up, cradling her in his arms. He took the steps two at a time. "Then why are we wasting time talking?"

"Thanks, Josh, I really appreciate it."

"No problem. Does Kelli know you're asking me to check up on her every night?"

"It's not checking up. Think of it as looking in."

"She doesn't know." Josh chuckled.

"She'd have my hide."

Josh laughed harder. "She already has that. Heard congratulations are in order."

"Thanks. I would like you to be one of my best men along with my uncle. We haven't set the date yet; that will depend on this trip."

Josh leaned back against the police cruiser and rubbed his jaw. "I know you love Kelli, she loves you, and I think you're perfect for each other. But are you sure about moving to Utah?"

"A man has to have a job to support his family."

"Kelli hasn't voiced any objections to moving?" he asked doubtfully.

"None. She's dug up more information on the state than their own chamber of commerce." Logan frowned briefly. "I've thought about staying here, but there aren't many requests for geologists in the local want ads." He looked over to where Kelli was helping the stage crew set up lighting and sighed. "I can't imagine Fairyland without her."

Josh stared at Logan as if he'd said something profane. "There won't be a Fairyland without her. Kelli *is* Fairyland."

Kelli stood in the middle of the bedroom and nervously ran a sweating palm down the front of the red satin nightshirt she wore. Logan had bought it for her soon after she'd explained why she always wore red. *Solitary Fairies* always dressed in red, while *Troop Fairies* wore green. Since she had started Fairyland alone, she'd decided she was the former and had begun dressing accordingly. With a nervous gesture she shifted a wrapped box behind her back. When Logan came into the room and closed the door she blushed.

Logan raised an eyebrow. "You sure did hurry out of the bathroom."

"I bought a going-away present for you."

He was more intrigued by her blush than by the idea of a present. "I don't leave for thirty-six hours."

Kelli took the brightly wrapped box from behind her back and handed it to him.

Amused, Logan studied the swirling lime-green and shocking-pink wrapping paper. He slowly slipped the canary-yellow bow off the package and ripped off the paper. Under two sheets of orange tissue paper he spotted his gift. Two pairs of satin boxer shorts, one boasting purple horseshoes, the other green shamrocks. "Oh, Kelli, they're fabulous. Where did you find them?"

"I had to drive all the way into Somerset to get them. Sadie Foster doesn't carry anything but straight Fruit of the Looms. She was quite shocked when I asked if she stocked satin boxers."

He sat on the edge of the bed and laughed harder. He had met Sadie Foster. The woman still thought saddle shoes and beehive hairdos were the height of fashion. With great care, he pulled the shorts from the box and held them up. "I love them."

"You're to wear them during the interview and they will bring you good luck."

"Which pair?"

"I'm not sure. I couldn't make up my mind, so I bought both." She gave the matter some serious thought. "You decide once you get there."

Logan looked at the woman standing in front of him and grinned. *Lord, how I love this woman.* He put the box on the floor and opened his arms.

She didn't need a second invitation—she flew straight into his arms. She heard his groan as he tumbled backward under her weight and smiled as she bent to kiss away the pain.

Ruth planted her hands on her ample hips and glared at her nephew. Logan was systematically destroying her once-gleaming domain. "Are you sure you know what you're doing?"

He glanced at the growing pile of pots and bowls. Silently he acknowledged that his aunt's question was justified. He was more comfortable with gravimeters and seismographs than with cooking. Since he was leaving in the morning, he'd wanted to make Kelli a special good-bye dinner. His aunt and uncle had been invited to a covered-dish dinner with a group of senior citizens, leaving them some privacy. Two frozen Maine lobsters sat in Kelli's sink on a bed of ice, and a pound cake was baking in the oven. Everything was going smoothly. He smiled confidently. "Piece of cake. How hard can it be to throw those two critters into a pot of boiling water?"

Ruth tapped her foot and glared at her nephew. "I wasn't talking about your cooking. I was referring to this job in Iowa."

"It's Utah."

"Same difference."

Logan knew the people who lived there would not have agreed.

"Don't you want to move to Utah, Aunt Ruth?"

"It doesn't matter to these old bones where they are, as long as they have a soft bed at night. It's Kelli I'm worried about."

"Why?"

"Because she won't be happy there," said Ruth. "She loves you and would follow you anywhere. But it won't be home for her. Didn't you see her face when she entertained those kids with tales of fairies and legends. She believes in them. She believes they live *here*."

He glared at the bowl of potato salad he was making. "What am I supposed to do? I have to work. Fairyland can't support this family, let alone a couple of kids."

Ruth's expression became dreamy. "Babies?"

Exasperated, he snapped, "Oh course, babies. We're talking long-term commitment here. Marriage, babies, orthodontists, and college tuition." He softened his voice and asked, "Wouldn't you like to hold a grandnephew or niece?"

"Oh my!" With a stubborn look she declared, "Fairyland is perfect for raising a family."

For the first time in his life, Logan lost his temper with her. "Dammit, Aunt Ruth. Money doesn't grow on trees. I want Kelli, Henry, and you to have the best. Our children deserve the best I can give them." He ran a hand through his already disheveled hair. "If that means moving to Utah, that's what we'll do."

Ruth blinked and gawked at her nephew.

Logan regretted his show of temper. It wasn't Ruth's fault he had spent a restless night tossing in his sleep tortured by dreams he couldn't remember. He opened his mouth to apologize when the cookie jar fell off the counter and smashed against the floor.

They stared at the scattered ceramic pieces and cookies, confused.

"You must have moved it too close to the edge," Ruth said.

The soft swish of the pet door caught his attention. He could have sworn all the cats were out. With an apologetic glance toward his aunt, he went and got the broom and dustpan. A frown creased his brow as he swept up the mess. He couldn't remember touching the cookie jar, let alone moving it.

After he'd returned the broom to the closet, he lovingly wrapped his arms around his aunt. "I'm sorry I yelled at you." He kissed the top of her head and gave her a gentle squeeze. "You could be right about Kelli, but I don't know what else to do. If we move to Utah, I'll buy her twenty acres and let her convert it into another Fairyland."

Ruth returned his hug. "You don't need to apologize. I was putting my nose where it didn't belong. I'm the one who's sorry."

"Nonsense. You have a right to voice your opinion. This move involves you too. We're family, and we're in this together."

She placed a motherly kiss on his cheek. "Sink or swim, huh?" Logan laughed and shooed her out of the kitchen.

Kelli sat back and groaned. "So that's what lobster tastes like."

Logan slid his arms around her waist and nuzzled her neck. "Ummm . . ."

She tilted her head to allow him more room. "It's the ugliest thing I've ever eaten, but it tastes great."

"Ummm . . ."

"Stimulating conversation we're having."

Logan laughed and stepped away from her. "I can't help it. I'm leaving in twelve hours."

Kelli pretended to pout. "You promised me dessert."

He quickly filled a tray with the remaining wine, two glasses, two slices of pound cake topped with Cool Whip and strawberries, and two forks. He turned off the light, leaving her standing in the dark. "If you want dessert, it's in the bedroom," he said as he left the room.

"Isn't that a little obscene?" she asked, following him.

A wicked smile flashed across his face. "Only if you tell."

She turned toward the stairs. "I wonder if this is what's known as having your cake, and eating it too."

"Dammit, Kelli. There's a strawberry stuck to my knee."

She giggled as she raised her head. "It goes with the Cool Whip in your hair."

Logan touched a patch of stickiness in his hair and grumbled something under his breath. Then he glared at the closed door, exasperated. "Why is Tinkerbell whining?"

"Strawberries are her weakness and she didn't appreciate it when you locked her out."

"Well, hell, she drank my wine."

Kelli reached over and scooped a smear of cream off his chest. She closed her eyes and sighed as she licked the white foam off her finger. "Stop whining, I shared mine with you, didn't I?"

He groaned as she licked her finger with her small pink tongue. Desire curled through him as he lovingly brushed at the crumbs clinging to the sides of her breasts. A gleam sparked in his eye as he spotted a crushed strawberry on her gently rounded hip. His white teeth flashed as he bit the fruit and tenderly licked the satiny skin clean of any juices. Logan lifted his head and studied the moist hip. Satisfied, he said, "You sure are a sloppy eater." He turned her over onto her stomach. "Are there any more berries stuck to your luscious body?"

Kelli gulped air as his lips touched the small of her back. "You started it when you put Cool Whip on my—"

His fingers teased the back of her knees and slowly made their way up her thighs. "Oh yeah, them. But didn't I get it off?"

Moisture gathered between her thighs and her hips rotated an invitation. "Didn't I get the strawberry that I'd dropped?"

Blood and heat rushed to heighten his arousal as he remembered exactly where the berry fell and how she got it. With rekindled desire he rolled her over and entered her with one sure stroke.

Her trembling thighs cradled his lean hips as

she arched to meet his thrusts. The tempo increased as need drove them forward, reaching for the zenith. His name tumbled from her lips as she attained her goal. He followed her over the edge with one mighty plunge, calling her name.

Minutes elapsed before he raised his head from the softness of her breasts. When his breathing returned to normal, he rolled over and hugged her to his side. "I love you," was whispered against her moist temple.

Kelli smiled and snuggled closer to his warmth. As sleep overtook her she said, "I love you too."

Logan threw his suitcase in the back seat and slammed the door. He had hurried through his shower and finished packing so that he could manage a few minutes in private with Kelli. But when he came downstairs the only people waiting for him were Aunt Ruth and Uncle Henry. They had wished him a safe and pleasant journey, and then handed him a note from Kelli.

"I'm sorry I can't look you in the eye and say good-bye. Let this morning's loving be my good-bye to you. You carry my heart with you. Dazzle them with your brilliance and hurry home to me. I'll be waiting. Love and Godspeed, Kelli."

Logan stared off into the surrounding woods. *Where in the hell could she had gone?* He didn't notice the narcissus or the yellow daffodils dancing in the morning breeze as he purposefully headed for the pond. She had ended her note with "Love and Godspeed." Who in their right mind used the word "Godspeed"?

He came to the fork in the patch and bore right. He heard her gentle singing before he spotted her. She was sitting in the grass with Caer's head resting in her lap. Today she was dressed in the same fairy outfit she had worn the day he arrived at Fairyland. Logan stopped and studied the bent head and crooked wings. There was a slight catch in her voice as she softly sang a lullaby. With a start of surprise he realized she was crying.

He shifted his weight and jammed his fists into the pockets of his pants. He wanted to go and comfort her, to tell her everything was going to be all right. But was it? Why couldn't she say good-bye? It was only a three-day business trip. He raised a brow as Caer gently nudged Kelli and turned toward him.

Kelli glanced over her shoulder and flushed. Logan stood there looking formidable in his gray business suit with his hands jammed in his pockets. She quickly swiped at the tears that had been rolling down her cheeks and stroked Caer. The swan looked between the two people, got to her feet, and waddled back toward her nest.

Kelli smoothed down her skirt as she stood up and nervously faced Logan.

"Why?"

"I'm a coward."

He was taken aback by her honesty. "About what?"

"Saying good-bye." She looked at the hurt in his eyes and tried to explain. "I've only said good-bye to one person in my life, and he never came back."

"Ben."

"Yes, Ben. At the end, we both knew he was going to die. When I said my first good-bye to a man who was dying, I promised myself I would never say good-bye to anyone I loved. I love you more than life." She looked at him tearfully. "How could I say good-bye to you?"

Logan wrapped his arms around her and held her tight. Moisture filled his eyes as she trembled against him. His voice was husky as he asked, "Didn't you ever say good-bye to anyone at the foster homes?"

"Only to the ones who didn't matter. If you formed a friendship with other foster children, they separated you fast. I made a friend once. Her name was Laura, and we were eight. We went everywhere together, we were inseparable. One day at school they called me to the office. A social worker was waiting for me. My bags were packed and in her car. They took me to another home in a different county."

"And you never saw Laura again?"

Kelli shook her head and blew her nose in the handkerchief Logan handed her. "So much for good-byes."

"What kind of social service system is that?" Rage boiled in him for the injustice a sensitive child like Kelli had suffered.

"The system is changing for the better. Today the social workers don't shuffle children through different houses. They feel it's beneficial for a child to make some attachments. They realize in many cases the foster parents and foster brothers and sisters are the only family they'll know."

Logan wiped at a smear of mascara she had missed. "I'm not going."

"Yes you are." She straightened his tie and patted his chest. "I can handle three days. I just can't say the words. They get stuck"—she gestured to her throat—"right here."

His smile was filled with love and understanding. "There won't be any more good-byes between us. I'll be back before you can say Rumpelstiltskin."

Kelli threw her arms around his neck.

He groaned and pulled her against his chest as he plunged his tongue into her mouth. He could feel the outline of her breasts pressing into the front of his shirt. Desire built and swirled in his stomach as he broke the kiss. "If I don't go now, I'm going to miss my flight."

"I'll walk you to the car."

"No, I want to imagine you standing surrounded by the trees with the pond in the background." He shook his head ruefully. "Lord, for the next three days I'm going to have erotic fantasies about a woman who wears wings."

"I think I'll picture you wearing strawberries."

He reached for her again. She clung to his shoulders for support until her knees became steady. With a tentative step backward she whispered, "Godspeed."

Logan lifted a brow. "Why Godspeed?"

"Why not?"

He chuckled and said, "Set your clocks for eight o'clock Saturday night. We have a date."

"I'll be waiting."

Reluctantly, he walked back toward his car. Turning twice he waved to the solitary figure standing in the bright morning sun.

Kelli smiled gratefully at Caer as she waddled away from her nest to share a quiet moment with a human. The swan laid her head back into Kelli's lap and hissed softly. Logan had just left and already she was lonesome.

With trembling fingers Kelli softly stroked the bird's sleek neck. What would happen to the swans and their babies? Could they survive the cold winter when the pond froze and food was scarce?

She made a mental note to ask Logan if they could find a home that had a pond. Maybe she could take them with her. She was already planning on taking Tinkerbell, how much more trouble could a swam family be? She wasn't sure about the cats. They seemed more at home outside wandering the woods. And she knew they preferred hunting over cat food.

What about the drama club? How would they perform their plays without a theater? Maybe she could donate that parcel of land to the school as a memorial to Ben. At the thought of Ben, tears gathered in her eyes. He loved this land and had passed that love on to Kelli. When he died and left a mountain of debts and back taxes, she had vowed to save the land.

She had kept her vow and saved it from foreclosure, only to lose it now to love. She wondered how she could sell the only home she'd ever known. And she wondered how could she not. She loved Logan to the bottom of her soul, and she understood his need to support his family. And he had to do that away from here. Still, he was proud of all that she'd accomplished. She'd supported herself for a long time. Now she would move on to a new phase in her life. She liked the idea of being cherished and loved by a man who wasn't afraid of responsibilities. She wanted to be able to spend time at home with her babies. She wanted to be a good wife and mother. If all that meant giving up Fairyland and moving, she'd do it without one word of regret.

A headache started to throb in her temples as she realized how much still had to be done.

* * *

Logan glanced at the clouds outside the window as the stewardess took away his uneaten lunch. He closed his eyes and pictured Kelli standing so alone by the pond as he walked away. She was a solitary fairy. She was beautiful with her golden hair coiled on top of her head, braided with rose-colored ribbons. Shimmering wings sparkled in the morning light and her lips were swollen and moist from his kisses. It had taken every ounce of willpower to walk to his car and drive away.

He shifted his weight uncomfortably in the luxury seat in the first class section of the plane. How was he going to manage three days without her if he couldn't even close his eyes without seeing her?

He forced himself to concentrate on the upcoming interview. He opened his briefcase and pulled out the latest company report. He read the first paragraph twice without remembering what he had just read. He pulled a pad and pen from the case and jotted down a list of things that would have to be done if he got the job.

The first item was to contact a real estate agent. He really should do that while he was there, just to get an idea of what was available. He figured he'd need about twenty acres, and the property better have a pond. Angus and Caer were going to have babies any day, so it should be a large pond. How difficult was it going to be to move an entire swan family? Would they survive in Utah? He made a note to call the local zoo to check on the best way to transport swans.

He wrote down Tinkerbell's name and then put a question mark next to the word "cats." They would need a large house with plenty of room for a growing family, and a guest cottage for his aunt and uncle.

With a sigh he read the growing list. He had just described Fairyland. What he needed was Fairyland transported across country. A headache started to throb in his temple at the list of things that would have to be done.

Eleven

Kelli answered the phone on the fifth ring. "Hello?"

"Did I wake you?"

Happiness lifted her voice. "Logan!"

"Who else would be calling you at this hour?"

She glanced at the kitchen clock. "No one has ever called me before at one o'clock in the morning."

"Good. Besides, it's only eleven on this end." His voice deepened to a husky whisper. "Miss me?"

"Immensely."

Logan paused and cursed the beige phone in his hand. He remembered the ad campaign, "reach out and touch somebody." He wondered if he could sue for false advertising. "How are Ruth and Henry?"

"Everybody's fine here. Ruth baked some brownies and Josh stopped by." She chuckled. "The man must be psychic; no one told him Ruth was baking his favorite. We played a game of checkers and he beat me."

"Is he that good?"

"No. I was that bad tonight. I couldn't concentrate." She wrapped her finger in the coil of the phone cord. "How has it gone so far?"

"Great. The top echelon wined and dined me while they grilled my socks off."

"What about your skivvies?"

"No, they left them alone."

Kelli laughed. "I meant, did you wear your good-luck ones?"

"The purple horseshoes did the trick. I dazzled them with my brilliance and convinced them they couldn't survive without me. Tomorrow they are taking me for the grand tour of the plant and field operations."

"Does that mean you got the job?"

"No, but I've got a good feeling about it. I'll wear the shamrocks just in case." He shrugged out of his suit jacket and removed his tie. "I'd better let you get some sleep."

"Okay, you be careful and knock them dead tomorrow." She smiled into the receiver.

"I will." He paused and said, "Kelli?"

"Yes?"

"Thanks for being there."

Her sweet laughter crossed the lines, gently wrapping around his heart. "Where else would I be but home?"

"I love you, good night," he whispered.

"I love you too, Logan. Good night and Godspeed."

Logan stared at the silent phone for a moment before replacing it in its cradle. *Where else would she be but home?* He unbuttoned his white shirt as he walked over to the huge plate-glass window and stared east.

With a heavy sigh, he turned and started to unpack his suitcase. As he lifted out a pair of pants a newspaper clipping fluttered to the bed. Curious, he picked it and scanned the headline. He dropped the pants back into the suitcase. Then he sat down on the edge of the bed and read the article.

His eyes lit up when he was done. The newspaper was from Pittsburgh and it was dated six months earlier. Excitement raced through him as he reread the piece.

Slowly lowering the crinkled page, he looked toward the window. "Well, I'll be damned."

Kelli tugged at Titania's wings and straightened the flowers in her headpiece. "There, all set. Just don't sit down."

Titania turned around and hugged her. "Thanks, Kelli. What would we do without you?"

The smile on Kelli's face slipped. "You would manage just fine." She glanced around the hectic backstage. "I have to find your court fairies. I promised them I'd do some last-minute alterations."

Ruth's gaze followed Kelli as she disappeared in the group of teenagers. Scowling, she bent and continued hemming Helena's gown. "You can stop worrying your hands, child, the skirt's finished."

Smiling, Helena looked down. "Thanks, Ruth. You're a lifesaver."

Ruth's reply was lost as someone across the floor wailed in distress. She glanced over to see the papier-mâché head of the donkey snag the sleeve of Hippolyta's gown. Ruth chuckled as the crowd of students parted and Hippolyta came running toward her. "Ruth, please, you've got to help me. That jackass tore my sleeve."

Lovingly, Ruth bent over and selected a yellow

thread, to match the gown. She blinked back tears of happiness. Lord, she had never felt so needed in her entire life. "Calm down, child. I'll have it fixed in a minute."

Kelli glanced over at the commotion and grinned. Ruth had handled it all like a champ. Every year the backstage jitters created total chaos, especially on opening night. Last year when Kelli had acted as wardrobe mistress, she'd safety-pinned everything.

She heard a collective, appreciative sigh from the fairy court as Puck arrived. Kyle Alman, the student heartthrob, was playing Puck, the mischief maker. His costume consisted of a holly leaf headpiece, silvery wings, and one very large diaper-styled garment. Kelli hid her smile and silently agreed with the fairy court. The seventeen-year-old youth would be devastating in ten years' time.

The thought of devastating males made her glance at her watch. Fifteen minutes till seven, that was quarter to five in Utah. What was Logan doing this minute? Did he get the job? Was he eating properly? With a shake of her head, she turned her attention back to the group of giggling fairies.

The Chinese lanterns blazed, signaling intermission. In her front row seat, Kelli stood up. "You two stay here," she said to Ruth and Henry. "I'll bring you back something from the refreshment tables. I don't want to see you get trampled by this crowd." She worked her way into the aisle and was swallowed up by the horde of bodies rushing toward the concession stand.

Logan shifted the pack strapped to his back

and searched the crowd. Where was she? With growing frustration he pushed against the flow of bodies, inspecting every scrap of red for the woman he had come home to. The seats were nearly empty when he spotted Ruth and Henry sitting in the front row. He hurried down the aisle. "Where's Kelli?"

"Logan! What are you doing here?" cried Ruth.

"I'll explain later. Where's Kelli?"

"She went to get us something to drink, son," said Henry. "Are we moving to Utah?"

He kissed his aunt's cheek and grasped Henry's hand. "Hell, no. We're staying here." Logan straightened and stared at the confusion at the rear of the theater. "You two enjoy the rest of the play. I've got to find Kelli."

Henry watched as Logan headed back into the crowd. With a smile he turned to his wife. "How would you like an old geezer to escort you to the refreshment area? I do believe we're about to be forgotten."

"I think you may have a point there." Ruth smiled and clasped his outstretched hand. "In your prime, old geezer, you could have given young Puck a run for his money."

Kelli and Titania were laughing as they ran through the woods with their skirts held high. They were going to make it! The Chinese lanterns were blinking a warning for everyone to return to their seats, intermission was over.

Before she had reached the refreshment tables, Titania had grabbed Kelli. Disaster had struck! Oberon, the King of the Fairies, had accidentally spilled a can of soda down the front of her gown, and Titania was in tears. Kelli had rushed her over to the house and run water from the kitchen sink over the stain. She had thrust a handful of tissues at the weeping girl and run upstairs for the hair dryer. Between the dryer and a steaming iron, the water mark was now barely visible.

They were racing around the back part of the stage when there was an announcement over the loudspeaker. "Would Kelli SantaFe please come to the stage area. We seem to have an emergency."

Dan Teeterman ran his finger around the inside of his collar and gaped at the wild man pacing in the wings. He had met Logan Sinclair on numerous occasions and he'd always seemed so helpful and pleasant. Now Mr. Sinclair was threatening to close down the play unless he found Kelli. Immediately.

Logan stared off into the crowd. No Kelli. Everyone was sitting, waiting patiently for the play to resume.

Kelli hurried to the far wing. What in the world had happened? She'd never heard anyone paged before. She glanced down at the front row and breathed a sigh of relief as Ruth and Henry happily waved to her. She had taken quick steps toward Dan, when she spotted him. "Logan!"

Logan heard her call his name and turned toward her. His breath slammed against his chest. She was a vision. She wore a dress with a long red skirt and a crisp white bodice. A silky red and white striped bolero offered her protection against the chill night air. Her golden hair flowed down her back.

She ran across the stage straight into his arms.

He absorbed the impact and bent to capture her lips in a heated kiss.

Kelli heard the audience applaud · and reluctantly broke the kiss. A fiery blush swept up her cheeks as she glanced out over the cheering audience. She buried her face in Logan's chest, praying the stage would open up and swallow them.

Logan blinked into the spotlights and smiled at the catcalls, whistles, and the calls for a speech. He picked up Kelli and walked over to the microphone Dan was holding. "Hello. For those of you who don't know me, I'm Logan Sinclair. Get used to seeing me around here. I'll be living at Fairyland with my wife." He lifted the woman in his arms higher. "Kelli SantaFe."

Kelli lifted her head from his shoulder and stared up at him. *Had he just said they'd be living here?*

But Logan was on a roll. "We'll be getting married here at Fairyland the first Saturday in June." When a roar of approval flooded the stage, he put Kelli down and bowed. "Enjoy the rest of the play, and thank you for coming." A resounding cheer went up from the audience.

"By the way," Logan added, "you are all invited to the wedding." Pandemonium broke out in the theater as he carried Kelli off the stage and disappeared into the woods.

Ruth swiped at the tears flowing down her cheeks. "Wasn't that the most romantic thing?"

Henry put his arm around his wife and hugged her. "Yes, dear. He must get that from his father's side of the family." He smiled as Ruth brushed his cheek with a kiss.

"I only have one question."

"What's that, love?" asked Henry.

"Why did he have a big sleeping bag strapped to his back?"

*   *   *

Kelli snuggled closer to Logan in the double sleeping bag and stared up at the stars. They were so bright she felt that if she reached out she could touch them. A contented smile curved her mouth. Logan had just taken her to the stars and safely brought her back. Her star traveler had returned home.

He felt her smile against his chest. "What are you thinking?"

"About the stars, you, and us."

Logan brushed the hair away from her face and placed a kiss on her nose. "I like your thinking."

She raised up on an elbow an stared down at him. "You do realize that you just invited an entire town to our wedding."

"It's a small town."

"There're over two hundred people!"

He leaned up and kissed her surprised mouth. "Be thankful we don't live in Pittsburgh."

She felt her nipples harden against the downy softness on his chest. She pulled back a few inches; she didn't want to be distracted. "You still haven't told me why you're here."

"I always wanted to make love in a fairy ring."

"Not here"—with a sweep of her hand she gestured fo the world outside their sleeping bag— "here."

Chuckling, he said, "Oh, that here."

"I can't believe they didn't offer you the job. They must be a perfect pack of morons. But don't worry, you're better off without them. You'll find something else, something better."

"They did offer me the job. I turned them down."

She was amazed. "Why?"

"You know why."

Kelli was silent. She knew she hadn't uttered

one single word against Utah. In fact, she'd gone
out of her way to encourage him. She had even
bought him good-luck boxers. Curious, she asked,
"What are you going to do now?"

Logan entwined his fingers in her silky hair.
"I'll be opening my own business in Somerset,
just like you knew I would." He trailed a finger
around her ear and down her jaw. "It's going to
be hard going for the first couple of years, but I
have a nice sized nest egg. The bulk of it will help
start the business, the rest is security."

She struggled to keep her mind on what he was
saying, not what his wandering finger was doing.
"Exactly what kind of business are you opening?"

Chuckling, he said, "You know."

Impatient at being told she knew everything,
when she was totally in the dark, she snapped,
"Humor me."

"The technical names are 'hydrogenation' or
'liquefaction.' It's the process used in converting
coal into a high-energy liquid fuel."

"Oh. Pennsylvania has a lot of coal."

His finger circled a pouting nub. "It's the wave
of the future. With oil and natural gas becoming
scarce, the government is pushing for fuel alter-
natives. The United States is the leading coal pro-
ducer, so it would be to our benefit to perfect the
process and make it economically feasible."

A moan escaped her as his fingers flicked her
rigid nipple. "So we can live here at Fairyland?"

"As you know, Fairyland is sitting on the
largest bituminous coal deposit in America."

"Why do you keep saying that?" she asked.
"How was I supposed to know about this hydrogenation stuff?"

Logan lifted his eyebrow and tried to see her

face clearly. "You put the newspaper article in my suitcase."

"What article?"

"The one about Congress's sudden push for alternative fuel sources. How this area of Pennsylvania has all the raw material and manpower, but is lacking the technical knowledge and research."

"Logan, I didn't put any newspaper article in your suitcase."

"Really?" He sounded surprised. "If you didn't, who did?"

They gazed into each other's eyes, trying to put an answer to his question. A gentle night breeze drifted through the trees, carrying with it a gleeful laugh, which no mortal could have made.

Epilogue

Logan dropped his briefcase on the kitchen table and stared at his wife. She was wearing green. "Kelli?"

She closed the oven door and smiled nervously. "You're early. Dinner won't be ready for another hour yet."

He stood transfixed, staring at the large bulky *green* sweater. It was an ordinary sweater with a rounded neck. The sleeves were pushed up her forearms and it matched the casual style of her jeans. But it was green!

For the first time in their eight months of marriage he didn't pull her into his arms to kiss her hello. He was too shocked. "You're wearing green."

Kelli anxiously tugged at the hem of the sweater. "You like it? I bought it today."

He unzipped his jacket and hung it on the rack by the door. He slowly walked toward her trying to read her expression. "Yes, I like it. Why did you buy it?"

"It was on sale," she said hopefully.

"I know you, love. You don't buy clothes just

because they're on sale. I practically have to force you to buy yourself clothes." He stood toe to toe with her and asked, "Why green?"

Kelli sunk her teeth into her lower lip and thought of the best way to answer that question. She took a deep breath. "Green is the color of *Troop Fairies.*"

"I thought you said you felt like a Solitary Fairy, and they wore red."

"I'm not alone anymore."

Logan gazed at the happiness in her eyes. "You haven't been alone for months. Why the sudden change?"

"You know I love you."

"I hate conversations that start with those words," said Logan.

"I haven't felt alone since you walked into my life. But for some reason you and I didn't seem like a troop. We were a couple, and I wasn't sure what category of fairies that fell under. So I stayed Solitary."

"And now?"

Her eyes were shining. "You did say you wanted some children."

"You're pregnant!" When she nodded, he beamed. "Yeah!" He picked her up, swung her around, and kissed her.

She opened her eyes and clutched the counter for support. "You are happy, aren't you?"

"How could you doubt that? I'm thrilled, excited, nervous, and scared spitless. It's wonderful." He leaned forward and captured her lips in another heart-stopping kiss. "How? When?"

"You know how," she chuckled. "I haven't been to the doctor officially, except for the test this morning. But as near as I can figure, our daughter will be born mid-September."

"Daughter? How do you know?"

"Call it intuition."

Logan placed his hand on her stomach. His baby was growing in there. He was going to become a father. Love radiated from him as he tenderly embraced his wife, the mother of his children. "I love you, Kelli Sinclair."

She nestled against his chest. Her voice was full of happiness as she asked, "Enough to buy me a whole new wardrobe?"

Logan's chuckle froze in his throat as the napkin holder fell off the counter. Bewildered, they stared at the scattered napkins and the wildly swinging pet door.

"Cats?" asked Logan.

"I could have sworn they were all outside," said Kelli.

"A baby is coming. A baby is coming," was shouted in the wind. Amidst the scurrying of little feet and cries of excitement questions were shouted and the call went deep into the forest.

"A girl baby. She said it was going to be a girl."

The wise one stroked his whitened beard and smiled. "She should know." At the gathering he raised his arms and commanded attention. "Come, children, we have much to prepare for. Babies aren't born on the wing of a prayer."

THE EDITOR'S CORNER

There's something a little bit forbidden about this month's group of heroes. For one reason or another they seem to be exactly the wrong men for our heroines to fall in love with—but, of course, the six ladies involved do just that, unable as they are to resist the potent allure of these special LOVESWEPT men. And what they feared was forbidden fruit turns out to be necessary to their very existences!

In **TROPICAL HEAT**, LOVESWEPT #432, Patt Bucheister creates a noble hero named John Canada, and she puts his nobility to the test by having him fight his overwhelming passion for Salem Shepherd, the woman he'd first known as a young girl. Together they had escaped from an orphanage and forged a friendship based on trust and need. But the feelings that began to surface in John as Salem blossomed into womanhood scared him, tempted him, thrilled him—and made him realize he had to send her away. Years later Salem returns to help John when his business is in trouble, and the feelings he'd once felt for her pale in comparison to the desire he knows he can no longer fight. These two people who've shared so much find themselves swept away on a current stronger than an ocean surge, right into the arms of destiny. Patt has outdone herself in crafting a love story of immense emotional impact.

Charlotte Hughes gives her heroine something of a dilemma in **RESTLESS NIGHTS**, LOVESWEPT #433. How can Kelly Garrett get on with her life as an independent single mom, when she discovers she's falling for Macon Bridges, a man who represents so much of what she's struggled to put behind her after her first marriage failed. Macon is the successful owner of the firm she works for; he has the tendency to want to take control and do things for her that she's just learned to do for herself; he's dedicated to his job and at times allows it to take top priority in his life. Then again, the man can charm the birds from the trees and certainly knows how to send Kelly's heart into flight! But

(continued)

once this smitten lady makes up her mind to risk it all on the sexy man who's causing her too many restless nights, it's Macon who doesn't stand a chance! Charlotte's lighthearted style makes this story pure entertainment.

TEMPESTUOUS, LOVESWEPT #434, by Tami Hoag, not only describes the feisty heroine in the book, Alexandra Gianni, but also the state of the atmosphere whenever she encounters hero Christian Atherton. The sparks do fly between the aristocratic charmer who is used to having women fall at his feet not throw him to the ground, and the lovely wildcat with the haunted eyes and determined ways of a woman who has something to hide. At first Christian sees winning Alex as a challenge, until he becomes thoroughly enchanted by the spirited woman he yearns to know all about. His wicked reputation seems in jeopardy as he longs only to soothe Alex's sorrow and shower her with tenderness. But not until Alex convinces herself she deserves to be cherished can she accept Christian's gift of love. This poignant romance features several characters from two of Tami's previous books, **RUMOR HAS IT**, #304, and **MAN OF HER DREAMS**, #331, the most notable character of which is hero Christian, whose love story you've asked Tami for in your letters. Enjoy!

Joan Elliott Pickart's **TO LOVE AND TO CHERISH**, LOVESWEPT #435, opens with a dramatic scene that won't fail to grip you. Imagine meeting a stranger in the foggy cocoon of night on a deserted beach. In a moment of yearning desperation, imagine yourself surrendering to him body and soul, then running off without ever learning his name! Heroine Alida Hunter was lost in her grief until she met the man with the summer-sky eyes. But she knew he was a fantasy, a magical gift she could never keep. Paul-Anthony Payton couldn't forget the mysterious woman who'd bewitched him then vanished, and he vowed to find her. She'd filled him with hope that night on the beach, but when he finally does find her, his hopes are dashed by her denial of what they'd shared.

(continued)

Alida's fear of loving and losing terrifies her and prevents her from believing in Paul-Anthony's promises. But the more she tells herself he's the forbidden lover of her dreams, the more Paul-Anthony makes her dreams become reality. Once again Joan delivers a powerful love story LOVESWEPT fans will treasure.

Judy Gill casts another memorable character in the role of hero in **MOONLIGHT MAN**, LOVESWEPT #436. Judy orchestrates perfectly this romance between Sharon Leslie, a gifted musician in whose heart the music has all but died, and Marc Duval, a man who's endured an unbearable tragedy and learned to find beauty and peace in the music he plays. Marc sees how Sharon is drawn to and yet tormented by the melodies he sends to her on the wind—as she is to his mesmerizing kisses. He knows she doubts herself as a woman even as he awakens her to pleasure beyond anything she's ever known. But until he can earn Sharon's trust, he can't know why she keeps turning away from him—and once she does trust him, he realizes he will have to confess the black secret of his own past. Caught up in the rebirth of the music inside her, Sharon revels in her feelings for Marc, but it all comes crashing down on her when she discovers the truth about the man she now loves with all her heart. Judy gives us a shining example of how true love conquers all in this wonderfully touching romance.

Fayrene Preston continues her SwanSea Place series with **JEOPARDY**, LOVESWEPT #437. Judging by the hero's name alone, Amarillo Smith, you can expect this to be one sultry, exciting, dangerous romance that only Fayrene can write—and you won't be disappointed. Heroine Angelica DiFrenza is surprised and intrigued when private investigator Amarillo, her brother's partner, asks her to dinner—the broodingly handsome detective had always seemed to avoid her deliberately. But when they finally end up alone together, the passion flares hotter than a blast furnace, and they both realize there's no going back. Amarillo couldn't deny

(continued)

what he'd felt for so long, but the time wasn't right. He was desperate to protect Angelica from the danger that threatened her life, and he needed a clear head and un-involved emotions to do it. But Amarillo's tantalizing kisses create a fever in Angelica's blood and the maelstrom of uncivilized hunger they'd suspected brewed between them rages out of control. You'll want to follow these two along on their journey of discovery, which, of course, leads them to beautiful SwanSea Place.

We promised you more information about our LOVESWEPT hotline, and here it is! If you'd like to reach your favorite LOVESWEPT authors by phone, all you have to do is dial 1-900-896-2505 between October 1 and December 31 to hear exciting mes-sages and up-to-the-minute information. You *may* call and get the author in person! Not only will you be able to get the latest news and gossip, but just by calling and leaving your name you will be entered into our Romantic Getaway Sweepstakes, where you'll have a chance to win a grand prize of a free week for two to Paris! Each call you make will cost you 95¢ per min-ute, and winners of the contest will be chosen at random from the names gathered. More detailed in-struction and rules will appear in the backs of our November, December, and January LOVESWEPTs. But the number will be operational beginning on October 1 and ending on December 31!

Get your dialing fingers ready!

Sincerely,

Susann Brailey

Susann Brailey
Editor
LOVESWEPT
Bantam Books
666 Fifth Avenue
New York, NY 10103